IN THIS WORLD OF ULTRAVIOLET LIGHT

STORIES

RAUL PALMA

INDIANA UNIVERSITY PRESS
INDIANA REVIEW

BLUE LIGHT BOOKS

This book is a publication of

Indiana University Press
Office of Scholarly Publishing
Herman B Wells Library 350
1320 East 10th Street
Bloomington, Indiana 47405 USA
iupress.org

Indiana Review
Bloomington, Indiana

Manufactured in the United
States of America
First printing 2023

Library of Congress Cataloging-
in-Publication Data

Names: Palma, Raul, author.
Title: In this world of ultraviolet
   light : stories / Raul Palma.
Description: Bloomington, Indiana :
   Indiana University Press, [2023] |
   Series: Blue light books
Identifiers: LCCN 2022027119 (print) |
   LCCN 2022027120 (ebook) | ISBN
   9780253064868 (paperback) |
   ISBN 9780253064875 (ebook)
Subjects: LCSH: Cubans—
   Fiction. | Cuban Americans—
   Fiction. | Miami (Fla.)—Fiction. |
   LCGFT: Short stories.
Classification: LCC PS3616.
   A33877 I5 2023 (print) | LCC
   PS3616.A33877 (ebook) | DDC
   813/.6—dc23/eng/20220614
LC record available at https://
   lccn.loc.gov/2022027119
LC ebook record available at https://
   lccn.loc.gov/2022027120

IN THIS WORLD OF ULTRAVIOLET LIGHT

BLUE LIGHT BOOKS

CONTENTS

IN THIS WORLD OF ULTRAVIOLET LIGHT

1

All along the Hills

We can still see Coach's headlights climbing into the hills. The way they pulse through all that brush reminds me of the old lighthouses back home off the Florida Straits, gyrating and gyrating. I don't know why we stand looking so long, especially since it smells like rain. We should be building the tent. Maybe it's 'cause we know that once those lights blink off, then we'll really be on our own.

Dark clouds and chimney smoke sail overhead. All this nebula offers only small and occasional windows to the stars. They're so bright out here. In this slick range surrounded by gringos or rednecks or backwoods white folk or whatever savages Coach said would lynch our Cuban American asses, we can hardly see each other. We're in a valley that is no more Georgia than it is one of the Carolinas. Ulysses, our team captain, twists on a portable lantern, unzips the tent bag, and dumps all the poles and nylons into the weeds. Then he orders us to get building. "Come on, you fat fucks," he shouts, which is a strange thing to say 'cause if anybody is heavy, it's him. Not that he looks grotesque. He's actually quite handsome, just heavy. The heavyweight, in fact. During season, he smiles and makes a spectacle when he drops so much weight because he can look down and see his little wrinkled wiener jiggling as he shakes his hips. When he does this in the locker room, the team cheers him on; they do not feel any shame in seeing him undressed or in chasing one another around the showers with towels. They do not see how easily things can go sideways.

* * *

I bet that Ulysses isn't too excited about camping with a bunch of JV wrestlers. He's done this whole team-building thing before. He was like me once: a rising sophomore, new to the sport. Clearly, he knows the drill. He takes out a Milky Way, Midnight Dark, bites off the wrapper, breaks off a piece.

"You have a chocolate bar," I say. "Holy shit. You got to share, man."

"Pass it around. Everyone gets a bite," he says and hands it over. So, I take a bite, let the malt nougat and dark chocolate dissolve on my tongue. Then I hand it over to Pedro, our super quiet and religious 156-pounder. He takes a bite and makes the sign of the cross. It's pathetic, really, the way all of us are crooning over this chocolate bar even as we kneel in the grass and dick around with tent poles. I'm probing my mouth with my tongue, seeking out stray deliciousness when Ulysses shouts, "Hey! Johnny, qué pasa, homeboy? Don't tell me you're allergic to chocolate too."

Johnny's our 103-pounder. I don't see him. It's because he's walked off.

Rafa, our 187-pounder—a rising junior who's already taken a state championship—pops up beside us like he's lookout. He peers into the valley, his hand as a visor keeping the moon out of his eyes, and he points to the woods. "Look! Dude's over there," he says. "You believe this guy?"

"Huevón," Ulysses shouts, "get over here." Then, because our captain has set the example, we all proceed to yell toward him too. It's like we're a bunch of ducks, quacking "huevón," caught in this vicious "huevón" sequence. But you know what? Johnny doesn't acknowledge us, so we stop. And what I think in that moment is that there's hope. Ignoring the bullies really can work out.

I see Johnny sitting in the grass, his tablet lighting up his whole face. He's so awkward, a pale Cubanito who keeps his head shaved; it makes him look like he's from another planet. He kind of is. Three years fresh off the boat, and he's got a face full of acne—pimples atop pimples. It's hard not to stare at the ooze or the deep scars or the white puss that bursts out and smears onto the mat.

From where I'm kneeling, the glow of the tablet seems to cast a halo over his egg-shaped head. Rafa kneels beside me, flips on his hoodie, and says, "Why's that ref even on the team? Right?"

* * *

It's always the tablet with Johnny. During season when we drop so much weight that focusing on anything becomes almost impossible, he manages to read. In study hour when most of us are sleeping so we don't think about the hunger creeping into our bones, he stares into that tablet like he's not even with us. He'll walk around school spitting into an old empty Gatorade bottle, posturing the tablet with his free hand. And during lunch when we wrap our bellies in garbage bags or Ziplocs or cellophane and sit out on the basketball courts baking in our sweats, trembling and eating ice cubes under the sun like a bunch of schizophrenic maniacs, Johnny lies on the court, his head on his backpack, and he reads, leisurely, like he could be on a beach somewhere, not starving.

Once, Coach asked us to write down our goals and then share them. Most of us said that we wanted to win state, go undefeated all season, get some scholarship or something. Rafa said he wanted to be on a cereal box. I was getting ready to joke about getting to second base with the cheerleaders—I thought it'd get a good laugh—but Johnny spoke up first. He said that he wanted to get a good score on the PSAT by the end of the season. And because his English was poor, it sounded, to some of us, like he'd said, "I want to score well on the *pussy eighty*."

We laughed. Even Coach said, "You know we're a wrestling team, right?" But this stuck with me. I thought, at the time, getting a good score would be quite an accomplishment for him—English being his second language. But nobody saw it that way. That exam had nothing to do with the honor and glory of the sport.

Rafa nudged me and said, "He's such an asshole. Sometimes I want to punch him in the face."

I feel sorry for Johnny because the guys really don't like him a whole lot, despite how talented he is as a wrestler. I don't know what training he did in Cuba, but he arrived in Miami skilled and ready for the mat. Coach went to great lengths to ensure he'd wrestle on our team. And if we wanted to make it to regionals, we'd need a strong 103-pounder, so we were all excited to have him. But somewhere along the way, resentment grew, and I don't really understand where it came from. I've seen, in those moments when Coach isn't in the locker room, how some of the wrestlers, Rafa included, will hold Johnny, pull down his shorts, and threaten to ice pick him—threaten to jam their fingers into him. This is where it always stops though. With threats. And Johnny standing alone, pulling his shorts and underwear up, then returning to his tablet like nothing has happened. It's terrible being in that locker room, knowing that the team can suddenly turn on you, on anyone.

So, when Coach said that he wanted to take the JV team into the mountains to weed out the sissies from the girls, Johnny stepped off the mat. He might have made it out of the practice room, but Coach noticed and asked Rafa to drag him back. And it wouldn't have mattered anyway. It's not like any of us had a say in the matter. It was our parents who loved Coach; they wanted us to be involved in the wrestling program—to stay away from drugs and guns and gangs. We would bond. Become men. That's what they must have thought. Not that Coach would leave us in a field with nothing but a few bananas and bottles of water. Nothing but a fishing rod, some tackle, and a tent.

* * *

Eventually, we figure out how to thread the poles into the nylon sleeves, and it all starts looking like a tent. Thunder rumbles across the valley. We're tired. We'd gotten on the road just after 10:00 a.m., and now this; the wind is really testing the integrity of our work. Nobody wants to be the person to say, "Look, guys, we've got to pull the stakes out and make sure the lines are tauter." I suppose we all know we've done a half-baked job, so when a hurricane-like gust manifests up on the hills—born for the sole purpose, it seems, of complicating our tent situation—we watch with concern. We see the wind shaking the tree branches violently, cascading down the hill and toward us. It crosses my mind that perhaps we should act. We should jump in the tent and anchor it down with our weight, but I only think these thoughts. Nobody takes any action. We just watch the gust slice through the valley, and when it arrives, our tent pops from the ground, then hovers like a child's kite and tumbles away.

It looks like it's running from us, zigzagging. It comes to an abrupt stop, only to lift off the ground yet again and tumble in an entirely different direction. None of us can anticipate its moves, so we have no choice but to run wildly toward it, wherever it lands. This hardly works. When the cloud cover obliterates all moonlight and the tent is lost, we understand, even though nobody really admits it, that we too are lost, enclosed by the hills and the clouds and the darkness and the very earth. The wind is cooler. It sprinkles, then rains. Ulysses shines his flashlight around, unsure how to proceed, and what we find, at that moment of great anxiety, is not the tent, but Johnny, sitting on a tree stump, the damn tablet lighting up his face. It appears he hasn't even moved to help us.

Rafa says, "I'm going to smash his fucking tablet," and he proceeds to march in Johnny's direction. Ulysses follows along with a flashlight, and I'm not sure if he's following to stop Rafa or to watch the pounding.

It's then that we catch a glimpse of the tent's reflective surface, caught in some branches and brambles. Ulysses shouts, "Everybody, we need to get a hold of it. Run!" So we do. But I do with some caution because I'm afraid that at any moment, it will tear loose and then we'll be searching again. With the gusts, the nylon expands and constricts. It looks like it's breathing. One gust tears it away from the brush, knocking me down into the mud face-first, and it would have tumbled away, but Ulysses grabs it with his free hand. And that's how we manage to salvage it.

I have to admit: staking the tent under such conditions is glorious. It almost makes all the trouble worth it. We celebrate with shouts and high fives and bro hugs. Ulysses squeezes me so tight. "You got mud on your face," he says, and he wipes some off. "Good job blocking." This praise, coming from the captain, makes me feel like I'm really part of the team. This is to say, spirits are high, but, as you've probably guessed by now, Johnny is having none of it. Where is he anyway? It's Ulysses who points him out to me. Johnny has shifted even further away from us. "What's up with homeboy?"

"He's like that sometimes," I say. "We shouldn't bust his balls."

"It's going to rain all night," Rafa says.

"I'm sure he'll be right over," I say.

"Yo. Yo, Johnny boy. You going to sleep in the tent tonight or what?" Rafa yells.

In response, the screen goes dark.

"What?" Rafa says. "He thinks he's invisible now. I see you, freak. I see you right there."

"Give him some space," Ulysses says, shoving Rafa. "Let's finish setting up."

* * *

After we load the tent with our bags and bodies, we rest. We lie there in a tent built for three people that is crowded with four. When the rain gets heavy and Johnny does peek in, we all scoot to make room for him. Even Rafa. But all Johnny does is toss his bags against the tent wall, then step out.

"Where the fuck is he going?" Rafa asks, loud enough to be heard.

Nobody responds. We listen to the rain and the thunder, expecting him to return, but he doesn't. "When his battery dies," Ulysses says, undressing to his camo boxers, "and he comes in here bored as hell, tell him he can sleep in the mud. Tell him to find his own shelter." The way he says it, I'm not sure Ulysses means it. He's frustrated, for sure. He lies down and curls against his bag to sleep. I close my eyes and try to doze off myself. I'm still hungry. And the tent smells like sweat and mud and bananas, but I must have fallen asleep at some point because I'm awoken in the middle of the night by hail, soft at first, but then vicious. In an instant, the canopy collapses over us, then rises.

A helicopter passes over the valley, momentarily lighting up the tent with the beam of a searchlight.

Nobody is awake; Johnny is still missing, evident by the gap on the tent floor.

All that unused space is tempting, but I don't inch toward it, even if I want to spread out and get more comfortable. I listen to the hail beating against the tent, much softer now. I watch rain seep in through the tears in the nylon, only little drops here and there. The way the wind is whishing about us, it really does feel like I'm back in the Florida Straits, listening to the sea, lost. Ulysses settles, turns toward me. Now he's resting his head on my bare chest. I can feel his beard brushing against my skin, the warmth of his breath. I close my eyes again and pretend that I'm asleep, and I think of Johnny wandering the hills, looking among the trees for a place to charge his tablet. It seems too easy: an outlet on a tree, male parts into female—the glow of a tablet in the dark woods.

* * *

I remember the first time I saw Ulysses. We were serving detention in one portable structure of the many littering the high school's field. It smelled of mold, and I had the sense that if I ripped off the wood paneling, that's exactly what I'd find, loads of it blossoming on the insulation. Already, a bit of mold was showing itself in the form of a water stain seeping through the discolored modular ceiling. I was in detention that day for something I'd rather not talk about. What's important is that he was there and that I was immensely interested in him in the same way that a cat eyes a new piece of furniture. I remember he smelled—or I should say reeked—of Cool Water cologne. One of his shoelaces was untied, and I thought it was so juvenile, almost charming for such a large man. He'd kick his feet back and forth and let that lace drag on the floor, which really bothered Mr. Phillips.

I hadn't joined the team yet, so I didn't know him that well. Sure, I'd seen Ulysses around the halls. Who could miss him? My first day at the school, it was he who opened the door ahead of me. He'd smiled and nodded in a friendly, bored kind of way, but I doubt he'd remember the incident.

In detention, he had a notebook out, and he kept drawing little pirate ships. Or he'd draw islands and maps where X marked the spot. I was so interested—and who wouldn't be under such circumstances? But I *really* was. Someone like Ulysses—I wouldn't have imagined this bend toward fantasy. As the clock pronounced each second, each minute, he kept working on these elaborate sketches, and I envied that he had something to keep him occupied. He was drawing mermaids and sea dragons and sunsets and pirates standing on schooners, but he must have felt me looking over his shoulder because he glanced back, and when we made eye contact, he closed the notebook. I thought, *Great. Now what do I do?* I wanted to see that notebook. I joined the team the next week.

* * *

In the morning, I sneak away to piss and eat a chunk of bagel I've smuggled from home. It's too small to share, and even then, it's soggy and has some lint on it. Do I feel guilty, hiding something from the team? Maybe a little. When I return, everyone is just waking up. I worry that they'll smell the bagel on my breath. That happens to me sometimes—I get paranoid. But nobody is paying attention to me. Nobody is paying attention to anything, including Johnny, who has been gone all night.

The valley's in such a state, it looks like it rained mud. I scan the hills and see only trees and brush. No sign of streets or electrical poles or anything that might suggest civilization, except for what looks like a small aluminum building at the crest of one of those hills. But it's too far to get to, hungry as we all are. Now and then, hang gliders launch from this structure. They're mesmerizing. They weave through the sky in brilliant yellows and oranges, which give life to the morning sky.

Ulysses acknowledges Johnny's absence. "Anybody seen the little guy?"

We scan the tree line. Nothing.

"Maybe the gringos caught him and barbequed him whole," Rafa says.

"Don't even joke," Ulysses says.

"Maybe the aliens came back for him," Rafa says.

"Come on," Ulysses says. "Don't be so hard on the guy."

"Sure. Sure. But imagine a whole planet of Johnnys. Fuck!"

"He'll show up when he does," Ulysses says. Then he suggests that we go to the bridge to wash and fish with the one fishing rod Coach provided.

We had passed the bridge when Coach drove in; he'd said at the time it'd likely be where we'd hang out all the time. "Some good fishing in my day. What do you say, Ulysses? Good spot, huh?"

To which he'd responded, "That's right. The spot."

But I don't want to walk through all this mud. A nice day like today, my idea of roughing it is sitting back and watching the hang gliders soar. But I'm not about to stay all by myself in gringo land. I've heard what those white folks do to people like us. Sure, it's all smiles and *how you do theres* and all that hick shit, but then you're getting comfortable and before you know it, they're chasing you across some unmowed field in their rusted pickups, big old Confederate flags waving around. No thank you. So I join my teammates even if our shoes are sinking deep into those muddy paths.

Ulysses is still in his boxer shorts. Shirtless, with the morning sun beaming over him, he looks firm and gelatinous all at the same time. I don't know how he's not cold. The rest of us are still in sweats, our towels hanging from our necks, a change of clothing in hand. We stink real bad—sweat crusted over sweat. It probably didn't help that Coach led a short practice session before we hit the road. We carry the kind of smell that gym uniforms get when they're kept in a locker for weeks and weeks. Even the bugs stay away. That's how bad it is. Rafa's holding the fishing rod and tackle box. Now and then, as we walk, he'll slap the back of our legs with the rod 'cause he's an asshole. Nobody says anything about it. We know he's egging us on, and giving him attention makes it worse.

Ulysses scratches his butt, then nearly slips in some mud. He steadies himself by taking down Pedro, who gets up, wipes the mud across his body; he doesn't act upset in the least. We push forward, and on the way to the bridge, who do we run into, tablet under his arm, big old sandwich in hand? None other than Johnny. It's more of a sub than a sandwich. Looks like it could have been a twelve-inch; it's got lettuce and everything spilling out. Earlier, I thought I'd smelled some vinaigrette, some red peppers, cheese. I thought I'd imagined it all.

"Do you see this?" Rafa asks. "Is that homeboy with a feast in hand?"

"It seems so," Ulysses says.

"Where'd you get that?" Rafa asks, poking Johnny in the chest.

Johnny takes a bite, then he tries to speak up. With all that bread and those bits of cold cuts rolling around in his mouth, coupled with his lousy English, we can't understand squat. In truth, I'm not listening to his words. I'm just watching him roll that food around in his mouth—such a little man, 103 pounds. He's not even half of Ulysses's size. And I'm thinking: greed. Yes. He's greedy.

Rafa rips the sandwich away from him, and I find that I'm not protesting. I know Rafa's actions are wrong, but what is Johnny thinking? Bringing all that food anywhere near a bunch of wrestlers trying to keep weight. Before Rafa can take a bite, Ulysses takes the sandwich, even if his hands are covered in mud, and he breaks the sub into pieces to be distributed equally among us.

And, God, it's a good sandwich, even if it's dripping in mayo and mustard. We stand there, eating our share, watching Rafa and Johnny push each other around, yelling all kinds of insults. Rafa, of course, is a bigger guy. Eventually, he loses his cool and pushes Johnny hard into the mud. Johnny's tablet slides out from his grip, but he's able to save it before it gets water damaged.

"You going to tell us where you got this food from?" Rafa asks.

"El piso, coño. I found it."

"You found it? No," Rafa says, "you're lying."

"I found it. Comemierda! Shit-eater!"

"Bullshit."

"Your mother," Johnny says.

"Even if you did," Ulysses says, "you weren't going to share?"

"No," he says, all matter of fact. "This is America, no? Not Cuba."

To this, Ulysses seems confused. "What about this being America?"

"Capitalismo, man! My money. My sandwich."

"I thought you found it," Ulysses says.

In This World of Ultraviolet Light

Rafa punches Johnny's gut, hard, and none of us do anything about it. Well, we eat. Johnny's on the ground, wheezing, and we stand around enjoying our share of the sandwich. I'm not usually like this. I know I should get up and check on the kid, but the sub tastes so good. The bread's nicely toasted, warm and crunchy, as if he'd just walked into a restaurant and ordered it, so we eat even as Johnny continues wheezing, even as Rafa goes on and on about how *This is a team! We're all brothers! We need to stick together! How can we win if we don't?*

"All right," Ulysses says, licking his lips. "Enough already." He checks on Johnny, helps him up. Then we continue down the path to find the stream, and Johnny follows along.

The guy seems pretty down in the dumps, so I fall back beside him and say, "Thanks for the sandwich," but he doesn't acknowledge me. He just powers up his tablet, and then he's lost in it, utterly absorbed, and I recall what Rafa always says: "He wrestles with us, but remember, he's *not* on our team."

*   *   *

I remember that when I joined, Coach made me try out. I didn't know I'd have to, and I didn't know I'd have to strip down in the locker room to weigh in. My weight class—something else I hadn't considered—was 145 even if I was weighing in at 149. Coach said I'd have to drop pounds. In any case, after I weighed in, Coach led me and a few other students to a windowless room, painted gold and blue after the school colors and covered in wrestling mats. It was there that I paired up with another 145-pounder, also new to wrestling. We were asked to line up, shake hands, then wrestle, even if we didn't really know what we were doing. It was a mess. What did I know? I kept giving my opponent my back because I had no technique at all. He pinned me in forty-five seconds, and Coach, clearly unimpressed, invited me to try out again the following year. How then did I make the team? Well, Jaime, who'd won, didn't have the grades, so you could say they were stuck with me. None of that matters. On that day, when I walked out, Ulysses slapped my ass and said, "Better luck next time." I smiled, thanked him, and walked out, acting like this was the most ordinary of exchanges, and later that night, as I was drifting off to bed, I swore that I could still feel the sting of his hand.

* * *

We arrive at the stream. The water's so cold that there's fog coming off it. I wonder whether bathing is a good idea, but then Rafa jumps in, and then it becomes a game: "Whoever doesn't jump in is a fag." So we undress and ease into the water. Between trying not to step on any sharp pebbles and navigating the cold current, I'm hardly paying attention to Rafa's stupid game until I see that Johnny hasn't joined us. I'd say for good reason. He has no towel. He didn't bring a change of clothing. He had no idea we'd be going to the stream to bathe. He's fully dressed, wanting no part in getting wet.

Rafa begins tossing pebbles, pronouncing each sentence with one. "Don't be a girl, Johnny boy. Get in the water. You smell like my father's farts." But this elicits no reaction until one of the pebbles lands right on the screen of Johnny's tablet. Expensive as those things are, the sound makes me cringe. Rafa stops with the pebble throwing. He doesn't say anything, but I'm sure he feels like he's gone too far. And Johnny, our little 103-pounder, inspects his tablet, then stands over the stream, glowering at Rafa like he could incinerate the motherfucker with his eyes. It's a difficult and awkward moment.

Ulysses breaks the tension. He ducks into the stream and then explodes out of the water. He puts his arms around me, lets his feet rise in the current. He's very warm. I like this warmth. I'm the only thing now keeping him from drifting away. He squeezes my neck and says, "Johnny's hiding something from us. Don't you get that feeling? Like he's got a serious secret. What's his secret?"

I nod.

"Like where did he go last night?"

"Oh. Yeah," I say.

"Johnny," Ulysses yells, "what's your deal? Where'd you go last night?"

He returns to his tablet, says, "Nowhere."

"He's a liar," Rafa says. "He's a fucking liar. Aren't you, Johnny?"

Johnny steps back. "Don't start with the pebbles again."

"I bet he's a fucking fag. Johnny's a fag. Look. He's not in the water. You a fag, Johnny?"

This is cruel. I feel it in my bones. Rafa doesn't even know what he's saying—the pain that such a word carries. Pedro laughs. So does Ulysses, and I find that I'm complicit in this too. Johnny looks to me like I'll defend him or something, but I shrug as if to say, *What? They're the animals.*

Rafa notices my gesture—the slightest shrug. He seems confused. I can see the seed of an idea forming in that hard head of his. In truth, I'm overtaken by fear. I don't want to be like Johnny, so I shout out in this grand performance, "Yeah! Don't be gay, Johnny." This pleases Rafa and the others. But Johnny shakes his head like he's disappointed in me. He moves further away from us and returns to his tablet, to whatever it is he reads.

The thing is, seeing him sitting there reading from the device, I realize that the battery should really be dead by now, and I tell my teammates. I explain that on the drive up, the only reason it didn't die was 'cause Coach let him plug it in to the adapter, which is major bullshit because he not only didn't let us charge our phones, but he confiscated them when he dropped us off. Gave us a quarter and a dime and a card with this number on it. Said we could find a phone three miles east if anything crazy came up. Said Johnny could keep his tablet 'cause he's a "student-athlete," whatever that's supposed to mean.

"He's probably going to take off again tonight to charge it somewhere," Rafa says. "I want to know where he goes."

"Why? Maybe he just wants some space," I say.

"Dude has no money," Rafa says, bobbing up and down. "I think he's up to no good."

"I doubt it," I say. "Johnny's so academic."

"What do you think, Pedro?" Rafa asks.

Pedro smiles. "I don't know, guys," he says and laughs. "Maybe we can train instead."

"Okay? Look. We're following him then," Rafa says. "He's got to juice up somewhere."

"Sure. I got no plans later," Ulysses says. Then he counts to three and sinks into the water, letting the current take him downstream. I lean against the bank, feeling the water cool me off.

* * *

All day, we take turns fishing and digging for bait. There are plenty of worms but hardly any fish. The berries we find in the vicinity look edible, but Ulysses isn't certain, so we resist the temptation. We eat the bananas Coach provided. Drink some of the water. Near dusk, when we've nearly given up, Ulysses catches one fish—a trout. He almost loses it when he pulls the hook from its mouth and raises it to celebrate. It slips from his hands and bounces around the rocks and mud. We chase it, trying to step on it, stop it before it plops back into the water. Rafa finally grabs it with my shirt, and we all cheer, except for Johnny. And I envy that about Johnny because what I really want to do is walk over to Rafa and say, "Did you have to use my shirt, asshole?" But I don't. I'm afraid of him.

We return to camp. With some persistence, Ulysses gets a fire going. He guts and scales the fish, drives a stick through its eye and holds it over the fire, turning it now and then. Watching it blacken, we begin to realize that this won't be enough to satisfy us. Somehow it looked larger near the creek. "What's the point of all of this?" I ask. "Sending us out here? Leaving us like this?"

Rafa shoves me. "Pondering life? What's the point of anything?"

"It makes you tough," Ulysses says. "Coach knows what he's doing. Months from now, when we're on the mat, fighting a pin, you'll remember all of this. And you won't give up. And years from now, long after you graduate, you'll be dealing with something tough, and you won't give up."

"I never thought of that," Rafa says.

"Coach is wise."

Now the smell of the fish is overwhelming. My stomach is rumbling. Ulysses breaks off pieces and distributes them. The meat is hot, but I'm excited to hold it. I savor it, separating spines with my tongue and spitting them out. We offer some to Johnny, who has not walked away for once. I give him credit. He's actually making an effort. He politely declines. "No. Gracias."

"What do you mean, 'No. Gracias'? Eat. You have to," Ulysses says. Johnny shakes his head, smiles.

"What are you smiling about?" Rafa takes some of the meat from Ulysses and presses it to Johnny's mouth. He grinds the meat into his face. "Eat," he says. "Eat."

Johnny falls back into the mud. He stands, steps away from the fire, and walks away.

"That was a bit much, don't you think?" I say.

"Much?" Ulysses asks. "That's the point of this. It's supposed to be too much. We're supposed to be so hungry, tired, anxious that when Coach rolls around on Sunday morning, we're willing to do anything for a fucking carrot. Too many sensitive people in the world these days."

"But if he doesn't want to eat, then he doesn't want to eat," I say. "We have to respect that."

"No. You're wrong," Rafa says. "He's mocking us. Coming out with that sub, knowing how hungry we'd be. Doesn't even pretend to want to share how he got it. Now he won't eat our catch!"

"I don't know," I say.

"You don't know whether I'm right, or you don't know shit?"

"Whether you're right, I guess."

"I thought you were smarter than that," Rafa says.

It's dark now. The last of the sun is slipping behind the hills. Ulysses rekindles the fire, stirs up the fish bones in it. He puts on a shirt 'cause of the bugs. Then we scan the valley, unsure of Johnny's whereabouts. When we've just about given up, the screen to his tablet lights up in the distance. "Motherfucker," Rafa says. "He'd rather read all weekend than hang out with us." He swallows his portion of fish, stands, and marches off in Johnny's direction. "Come on, y'all."

"You thinking what I'm thinking?" Ulysses asks. "Come on, guys."

I'm still sitting, sucking fish grease off my fingers, and they're all marching out toward the hills. Even Pedro. At first I don't plan on joining them. I look for bits of discarded fish around the fire. I thrust the fish head out of the tinder and drink the juices, even while the head burns my fingers. But then I hear a radio come on in the distance, blaring "Old Country Road," and I get this image of old white dudes sitting around a fire, cowboy hats and all, and I run off with the others.

* * *

Johnny's crossing the bridge when we catch up, or it appears to be him. The sun has set, and it's hard to see much of anything. But he stops and the tablet lights up, and then we're certain it's him.

"Guys," I whisper. "Don't you think this is getting a little out of control?"

At this, even Pedro laughs. "Come on, dude. The guy's asking for it."

"Asking for what, exactly?"

Rafa puts his hand on my shoulder and says, "We're just following, okay?"

"Okay."

"I mean, aren't you curious?" Rafa asks.

"Yes. Yes. I am."

"Then let's go," Rafa says, proceeding. "He's on the move."

We follow Johnny over the bridge and onto a gravel road, and we walk for a long time, passing a few old mailboxes and garbage bins along the way. The whole time, Johnny's just walking straight, not like someone lost or exploring, but like someone certain of their destination. And the further we walk, the more out of sorts I feel. We encounter no cars, no people, no animals. The road might as well cut through some wasteland. The only life we see is the glow of some porch lights up ahead. It's a small cabin with a wide driveway and an exposed stone chimney. We can smell the chimney smoke now, strong and fragrant. Light is spilling out toward us, casting the trees long and thin. I'm half expecting to find the traditional Confederate flag, the customary tree with the limb large enough to hold a man's weight, the trio of men in camo sitting on the porch, cleaning their guns. But I don't see any of that, and what I do encounter surprises me. Near the road, there's a small plaster grotto with a replica of the Virgin Mary holding her baby. Here, Johnny does pause. He kneels before the statue, sets his tablet down, and produces the sign of the cross. After a prayer, he proceeds further along. "Would you believe that?" Rafa asks. "The little fucker believes in Jesus."

"And?" Pedro says.

Once we're certain that Johnny has moved up ahead, we approach the altar. There are devotionals surrounding the effigy, a loaf of rotting bread, pennies submerged in flooded trays. It all smells of old, damp cigars. Etched into the plaster are names: Arturo, Jaime, Jessenia. The Virgin herself is bleached white, though it's clear from some of the light-blue cracks on her gown that she must have been painted at one point. I'm used to seeing the grotto adorned with starfish and lilies, not this way with ribbons and pins and dead flowers. "Look at this shit," Rafa says, kicking pebbles toward the altar. "I don't know how, but we walked through the woods and found Hialeah."

"Be respectful," Ulysses says, pausing for a moment. He kneels, bows his head, so I kneel too, only I don't pray. I can't. For one thing, I keep hearing Rafa pacing around behind me, and so I'm worried he's going to do something stupid, like shove my face into the statue. I've seen him do shit like that before. I've seen him, in the lunchroom, shove some kid's face into a slice of pizza. In addition to that, there's a feeling that I'm getting, like my stomach is digesting itself. I'm so fucking hungry. The fish helped, but if I don't eat something soon, I don't know what'll happen. Even now, looking down at the bread all rotten with green gunk—I want to bite it. I know better, but I want to.

* * *

When I joined the wrestling team, my father was so proud. I was too. He took me out to lunch one afternoon—just the two of us—and he told me stories from Cuba when he used to wrestle. I ordered a mahi-mahi sandwich, and he ordered a seafood pasta. Even though we were sitting out there at some riverside restaurant, waiting for our meals, he insisted on showing me some of the moves right then. I'm sure the patrons must have gotten their money's worth, watching him pull half nelsons and arm bars and single-leg takedowns on me, right by the table. Still, it was nice to see him light up that way, and when the food arrived, he mellowed out a bit, and he said something that has stuck with me: "Now that you're on the team, you're really a man." I guess it was meant as a compliment, but it made me wonder: *Did he think I was any less of a man before?* Look. I get it. My father grew up in Havana during a time when certain kinds of soft men were rounded up and put in prisons, deemed mentally unstable. He'd made his position known. Once, when I was quite young and playing with my sister's dolls, he ripped them away from my hands, and he said, "No boy of mine will play with dolls." It seemed extreme. As a child, I didn't understand it, but I felt the shame. For some time after, I thought of him as nothing more than another conservative, but now I wonder, was it his love that he was expressing, his fear of what could happen to me if I didn't grow up to become a strong man? I don't know, but what I do know is that at the fish restaurant, he seemed free of some anxiety; it was as if my relationship with him was, just now, really beginning. When my sandwich arrived, I didn't touch it. I wasn't hungry, or, rather, I wasn't hungry any longer.

* * *

In stopping to admire the altar, we lose Johnny, so we hurry up along on the road, and after some time, we see an old gas station. I'm not sure it's functional. It seems, in my estimation, like it's been reclaimed by the woods. The pumps are busted. Some nozzles are wrapped in plastic. There's a small pine tree growing from one of them. And there's a sign on the ground that reads, "Future site of Texaco Gasoline," but the sign looks really dated. The convenience store's front doors are secured with chain and padlock, and the large glass pane surrounding the doors is partly shattered, freshly shattered, it seems. I'm sure we would have kept walking along the path, but then we see the glow of the tablet inside the store. Rafa grabs my shoulder and says, "Look! The motherfucker's in there."

"I'm not going in there," I say.

"Oh, you're not?" Rafa says, like he plans on making me.

"Why is he here?" Pedro asks. "This is weird, guys."

"Because," Rafa says. "He'd rather hang out in this shithole than with us?"

"So now what?" I ask. "Are we satisfied? Can we get out of here now?"

In This World of Ultraviolet Light

"Dang!" Ulysses says. "Doesn't it feel like we're in one of those zombie shows? We should check the store to see if there's any canned food or anything, really. Maybe we'll find some old beer."

Ulysses is the first to step through the glass threshold. Once he's in, he helps us get through. Inside, it smells like mold and oil. Ceiling tiles are swollen and dripping. The shelves, unfortunately, are cleared. It's all dark except for the glow in the back corner. And there's this beeping sound—beeps every few seconds. "Johnny," Rafa yells. "We know you're in here. Come out of hiding?"

The glow of the tablet goes dark. Ulysses gestures toward the shelves, and we split up, moving down each aisle slowly. It occurs to me, then, that each of us are wandering the store for very different reasons. Rafa first checks the cashier's box. I hear him messing with the register, but he must find nothing because all he does is take an old metal garbage bin and beam it at the partially shattered glass. Glass cascades on the floor. "Hey," Ulysses shouts. "We don't need to be making so much noise, or you want to get caught?"

At this, Rafa says, "Don't be paranoid. Nobody's coming."

I check the bathroom, half hoping I'll find a few rolls of toilet paper or some soap—all things I did not bring along on the trip. When I open the door, the light turns on automatically. There must be a sensor, but I'm surprised by the light. I didn't think such an old place would have electricity. But there's nothing in the bathroom, just tons of cobwebs and a broken toilet. "Guys," I say. "I think this place is connected to the grid. Look!" I prop the door open so we can see better.

Pedro and Ulysses search the freezer, but they find nothing but empty milk crates and a dozen or so bottle caps. And once we're certain there's nothing useful in the station, I suggest, "Maybe Johnny's not actually here. Maybe he went elsewhere." The truth is, though, I know he's there. Because while Rafa moves up and down the aisles, kicking at the displays and making a real raucous, I glimpse the cord of Johnny's charger. It's plugged into the wall, and following it, I can see where Johnny is hiding—behind a shelf that's been pressed up against one of the walls.

And maybe we would have moved along further that night, but then Pedro finds the cord. "Look, guys," he says, lifting it up. Rafa comes running over, and he follows the cord to the shelf. Then Rafa and Pedro flip it over, violently, revealing Johnny. He's lying there on the floor, wrapped in a blanket he got from God knows where. He's covering his body, anticipating a beating.

Rafa kneels by his face and says, "Are we really that bad? You have to hide here like a fucking rat?"

"Guys," I say, "I think he just comes here to charge his tablet. It's not like that."

Johnny nods, shows us the cord.

"Bullshit," Rafa shouts.

"Guys," he says, "I got to study. It's nothing personal."

"Study, huh?" Rafa says and reaches for the tablet. "Let me see that."

Johnny recoils, holds his tablet closer, so Rafa kicks him and then rips it out of his grip. He kicks him hard, and now Johnny is wheezing again, his cheek flat against the station's flooring. I want to kneel beside him and check to see if he's all right, but everyone's in the way, and Rafa's making a real show of it all. He's looking through the tablet and laughing and laughing, and Ulysses and Pedro are piling up beside him, saying, "Let me see. Let me see it too."

But Rafa doesn't let them. Not at first. He's laughing and acting cryptic, and he says, "You don't want to see. Trust me."

"Come on," Ulysses says.

"This ref said he was reading. Want to see what he was reading just now?" Rafa shows us the screen. There's a picture of a dark-haired woman, her lips plump, red, her breasts firm, leathery, her nipples dark irregular ovals, one pierced. She's pushing her chest out, leaning against a wall. In the background, there's a vast ocean, some palm trees. She's muscular. Her abs are chiseled. There are veins running down her forearms, and she's holding her flaccid junk in her meaty hands.

"Damn," Ulysses says, "I think I'm going to start reading too." He says this before he's processed the whole photo. Then he notices it—the hood drooping over the penis, and he's really dramatic about it. He punches the shelving and everything. "Fuck! That's some sick shit. Why you set me up, Rafa?"

Rafa's having a good old time. "Something you haven't told us, Captain? You into this like Johnny here? You can look at the picture longer if you'd like," he says, handing over the tablet. "Look, I can even zoom in if you want a closer look." And Rafa does zoom in.

He shoves the tablet in all our faces, and Ulysses just keeps saying, "Fuck. I was looking at the tits. Turn that shit off."

Now, in all the commotion, Johnny is sitting up. His sweater is caked in mud. He's tense. He seems so delicate under his blanket. The guys are all caught up with the tablet; they've left Johnny with an opening. He darts toward the door, only Rafa trips him before he can get away. Johnny tumbles into more of the shelving. "We're in the middle of nowhere," Rafa says, standing over him. "Where does this guy think he can run off to? More importantly," he continues, "we have something we're going to have to deal with as a team. How do we kick the fag out of our hundred and three?"

"Stop," Johnny says, standing up. "This is a misunderstanding."

"Of course," Rafa says. "Just like you found that sandwich this morning."

* * *

Rafa drags Johnny out onto the road, pulling him over the broken glass and the pavement. At first Johnny keeps trying to stand and run off, but between Rafa and Ulysses and Pedro, he can't get away; they keep pushing him toward the camp, and this continues until Johnny seems exhausted, at which point he just lets us shove him down the road. Sure, there are times when Johnny suddenly springs to life with newfound energy and tries to run away, but there's no escaping.

Occasionally, Rafa messes with the tablet, pulling up new tabs, new photos, showing off every penis he finds. But there's this one photo. Real fucked up. Rafa comes across it as we're passing the altar. It's in black and white. At first, it looks like shoes and belts and shirts and all kinds of discolored clothing, but when I look closer, it's bodies. Human bodies. They're thin and frail, dead looking, and piled atop each other. I don't know for certain, but I understand the photo to be of a death camp. "I don't find this even a little sexy," Rafa says. "What's this all about, Johnny?"

And with the question posed, Johnny throws himself before the altar of the Virgin. He lands on his knees, displacing many of the devotionals. He puts his arms up and says, "Por Dios. Déjame."

Rafa and Pedro grab his legs and drag him back onto the road. Johnny's digging his fingers into the ground, and, in the process, the Virgin tumbles onto the road and shatters. We're getting ready to lift him up and continue walking down the road when we notice a figure standing at one of the cabin's windows. The lights on the porch flip off and on multiple times. "We got to dip," Rafa says.

Ulysses tugs at him to come along, but it's here that Johnny makes his stand. He drives into Ulysses with all his might—junior varsity 103-pounder against our varsity heavyweight—and to our surprise, Ulysses tumbles to the ground. Then Johnny mounts him and proceeds to pummel his face. It takes a moment for Ulysses to gain his bearings, and when he does, he swats Johnny off.

"Give it to me!" Johnny shouts, pointing toward the tablet.

"This?" Rafa asks. Then he smashes it on the floor.

"Cabrón! Why'd you do that?"

"Guys," I say. "No more of this. It's out of control." Nobody hears me, so I say it louder, this time standing between Johnny and the others. It feels right, standing up for my teammate. I look over to Johnny as if to say, *I've got your back. I'll help you, okay?*

But he's not responsive. He's just angry, and he comes at me and punches me right in the gut, and he shouts, "Fuck all of you." And with that, he walks away. He doesn't run. He just walks off into the dark, leaving his broken tablet behind. I like to think that he gets away because everyone is laughing at me for getting punched.

* * *

When we arrive in the valley, short one teammate, the fire has burned out. We sit around it anyway. Red and blue lights move through the hills; the absence of their siren is eerie. I keep thinking about what Coach said and about our Cuban American asses getting lynched. Even though Johnny hit me, I worry about him out there. I worry about us too: "You think the police are looking for us?" I ask.

"For what?" Rafa asks.

"For vandalism. For fighting."

"Nah. You think police really care about those things?"

In This World of Ultraviolet Light

Ulysses is pouring water over a cut on his knee. I take out some tissues from my bag and help him clean up the blood. He rubs his hand through his hair, exhales. "I don't know. As far as I'm concerned, if anybody asks, we didn't do anything. We're just wrestlers on a camping trip."

Rafa's going through the tablet, giggling to himself. Even though he smashed the screen, it still powers on. Now there are fragments of images, bodies shattered, a hybrid of parts. He seems fascinated by this. He's such a child. He mouths, "Palm trees, boobs, words, hair, colors, numbers."

"Don't you think you should shut that off?" I say.

"True. Shut it down," Ulysses says. "They'll see it."

So Rafa does. He sits next to Pedro, puts his arm around him, and says, "You gay too?"

"Don't touch me, man!"

"Who do you think is the cutest?" Rafa asks, clearly just egging him on.

Now, the police lights are at the base of the hill—high-powered lights that blast onto the valley. They must be looking for us. I've got my hand on Ulysses's thigh, cleaning up all the blood that's dripping down. I rub deeper on his thigh, and he shudders, but then he relaxes a bit. He's looking at me, watching me clean the blood that's dripping now into his shorts. I want him to know what's going through my mind. The way he avoids my gaze while also looking at me gives me this feeling that he knows. I'm not sure. Not at all. I want to feel him out, so I say, "X marks the spot."

"What?"

"The maps. The treasure maps. I saw you drawing them in detention."

"Oh," he says. "I love that shit. Pirates and all that. You like pirates too?"

"Sure. But let me get this straight. Wrestling is not your life."

"It's my life," he says. "During season."

He smiles. I look at the Kleenex now. It's all red. He's hardly bleeding anymore. I pour some more water over his knee, pat his leg. I don't know what to say next. "Thanks," he says and smiles.

This means something. Or maybe it doesn't. I'm terrible at reading these situations. I touch his thigh again. Then the beam finds us, and we separate. It lingers there for a moment. Rafa waves, gives a thumbs-up, and smiles. We all wave. We can't see who's shining it, and we're not sure what kind of trouble we're in. A voice shouts, "You boys seen some Mexicans running around these parts?" We say that we haven't, and to our relief, the beam moves on, scanning the valley, gyrating.

2

Ropa Vieja

I

Two years ago, a local Cuban radio station pronounced Fidel Castro dead "at last," and I remember thinking at the time: *That's a bit harsh, isn't it?* The news broke on my commute to the Doral Chamber of Commerce, and somewhat new to Miami, I wasn't prepared for the significance of such an event.

In fact, I switched the station and drove as if it were any ordinary day in beautiful sunny Miami. But by the time I made it to Hialeah's Forty-Ninth corridor, a mere twenty minutes later, it was clear that I'd be late to work, again. And I'm not talking about the usual traffic. There's always traffic on Forty-Ninth Street. What I saw were people leaning outside their car windows banging pots and pans and shouting, "Viva Cuba!" It was unbelievable. All along the sidewalks, families were parading and waving Cuban flags. Already, there were cardboard signs proclaiming "No Mas Exilio" and "Tu Día Llego." Who'd had the time to make signs? I was astounded, especially, when just two car lengths over, a shirtless boy set off a series of fireworks, which sparked and crackled and scared the life out of me.

Offices emptied early. High school students skipped school, went to the beach, made love along the shore. In bakeries all over town, people huddled together, laughing and toasting with Cuban coffee to independence. Calle Ocho shut down where it intersects with Versailles Cafeteria; local sweat-covered commissioners stood on the hoods of cars outside of the café walk-up window, ties flapping in the wind, proclaiming, in Spanglish, promises of a new future for trade between Miami y Cuba. For many Cuban exiles, the chance to see long-lost relatives seemed a possibility. There would be no more braving the Florida Straits in makeshift vessels. Elián González would return to his rightful family in Little Havana. Nurses and paralegals in America would transform into surgeons or attorneys overnight. There would be the reclaiming of land divided among a people. I met up with my buddy Chencho at one of those cafeterias. Sure, I didn't understand any of it, but it was a good time nonetheless, and while I sipped on that Cuban rocket fuel, he romanticized how Cubans all over the world would finally sleep under the warm embrace of home. They could return to their native soil, see their families, and never leave the island of lizards and frijoles negros again.

But Castro hadn't died. A few days later, the man delivered a heavily televised speech in La Plaza De La Revolucíon just to prove it, and Castro seemed to take great joy in holding up a copy of an American newspaper declaring him dead; he was wearing his signature military uniform, faded from deep evergreen to an olive; he looked sick, his skin blotched and his voice wavering. I couldn't follow his speech. For a while, he used tobacco leaves as a metaphor for his life. Somewhere between hanging the leaves to dry and the lighting of the cigars, Castro lost track of his thoughts.

Chencho was in my office, as he usually is, helping me decide on the catering menu for my next Doral Chamber of Commerce fundraiser when the broadcast came on. He pulled his white handkerchief from his suit pocket and threw it at the floor. "That piece of shit will live forever."

* * *

Born and raised in Chicago, I'd never given Castro any serious thought. My concerns were with baseball, not world politics. I grew up blocks from Wrigley Field. I'm kind of a *major* Chicago Cubs fan. So, when Chencho would complain to me about Castro, I'd nod along, remembering the Billy Goat Curse, the years of championships stripped away from the Cubs' franchise. Baseball, really, was the only way I could make sense of the whole thing: what it felt like to be robbed of a possibility. Yes! I could relate. All over the world, fans decried the curse—prayed, just like me, for its end.

In this way, I understood Chencho. Cuba had been robbed of a promising future. Castro had prevented business, industry, American cooperation, all in the name of some cursed Stalinist revolution. But I have to say, I also found Chencho to be somewhat unreasonable. Maybe it's because he was a Republican—the kind of guy who voted for W. twice. While, sure, I didn't know a lot about Castro, I did know some things about Cuba. One of my English professors at the University of Chicago had taught me that in Cuba, health care was free; people lived long lives. Children had access to quality education; the country's citizens were avid readers—such a small country, yet one that came to the aide of other countries in the face of great injustices. I'd hear Chencho talk about all the great injustices of Cuba—conflating Clinton with Castro— and, of course, I was skeptical. Castro couldn't be as bad as Chencho had said. Che Guevara and Castro were friends, after all. And though I never dared to admit it, I always wondered why Cuban exiles hated someone as bold and inspiring as Castro. He looked like the kind of kid who always wanted to grow up and parade around town in make-believe military uniforms, and he'd done it. He'd come out from the mountains and made his dreams come true; it doesn't get more American than that.

So, when Chencho tossed his handkerchief on the floor and said, "That piece of shit will live forever," I leaned against my desk and said, "But look at him! He could be your grandfather." Then feeling as though I'd made a good point, I paced around the room and said, again, "Look at him!"

Chencho didn't. He gave me *the look*—the same one he'd given me some months back when, after spending all week acquiring stone crab for our legacy event, I suddenly suggested that perhaps something like burgers and fried chicken would suit the stakeholders better. *That look.*

He finished his coffee, returned to his office. Then just as I was settling into my seat, preparing to get a grip on my inbox, he popped back in and shouted, "My grandfather?" In truth, I was a bit taken aback by Chencho's tone. I was his supervisor, after all. Back in Chicago, would I have let my subordinates speak to me that way? No! But this was Miami. I knew that. The flavor was different. Cubans had a way about them. "You want to talk about my grandfather?" Chencho said, taking his empty Styrofoam coffee cup and crushing it in his hand. "Well, my friend. My abuelo rotted in jail for ten years because of that son of a bitch. So, forgive me if I'm upset about it."

"Look, Chencho," I said, "people go to jail for a reason."

He laughed. "Yes. Yes," he said. "I'll promise you this. When that piece of shit dies, I will host a feast in my home. Best Cuban food you will ever taste. You're a Yankee, y tu no sabe; you would hardly understand, but I will ask you to join me so you can see. And you will see, I swear on my Tía Rosa, just what a piece of shit that desgraciado is. You will see it, okay? You'll come?"

"If you're cooking, I will be there. Of course!"

"One day, my friend. Maybe you'll finally get lucky with a nice Cuban girl. Even ugly gringos like you could get lucky when that bastard dies," Chencho said, and he returned to his work.

* * *

When Chencho calls me ugly, it's a term of endearment, or so I think. He's no Don Juan himself; he's bald as a baseball with thick eyebrows that intersect above his nose, but he's a respectable man, especially at the events when he's got his chef's hat and apron on. People

In This World of Ultraviolet Light

love Chencho for his good cheer—the way his laughter can spread through a crowd and bring joy to all there. I've come to know him quite well during my time at the chamber. He was born in a small town just southwest of Havana, named Guanajay. I love that name; it sounds like something that would go good with rice.

Up until the age of sixteen, he lived on a tobacco farm that his uncle Guicho operated; it was near some mountainside resort where Spaniards came to soak in salts and die under the palm trees. For Chencho, his time in Guanajay was idyllic, spent catching lizards, playing chapitas with the neighborhood kids, and, occasionally, sneaking into his uncle's tobacco drying house with la vecina.

The drying house stood in a sea of tobacco crops that spread up the slope of a tree-filled hill. It was an old stone structure with a dark wooden roof that was always splotched in bird shit. Its doors were never locked. Hanging from the ceiling, most of the year, were the long, sweet leaves of tobacco, bunched and browned by the process. And there were seldom flies in the house, he'd said, just rats and stray cats here and there; it seemed the only place that wasn't afflicted with flies.

Chencho loved talking about that drying house. "Sometimes," he'd say, "the tobacco leaves looked like old, browned laundry, twisted and hanging from the ceiling, only nice smelling." But, certainly, there must have been times in the year when the leaves were old and brittle. During these moments, he must have looked out at the still-growing crop, knowing that it too would be hung from the ceiling soon; it too would lose its color. In time, the dried leaves would be taken down and rolled and shaped into cigars and distributed across the world and incinerated and smoked or stored and revered—distributed all over, that is, except for the United States. We have an embargo in place, though I'd be lying if I didn't admit here that, sure, I had a few Cubans back in Chicago. *Why not?*

Once, Chencho got a job at one of the Spaniard's resorts. He'd never seen a pool before. Who would have thought that communism would equate to *no more swimming pools?* But the resort was different—funded by a man who still lived in Spain. And as much as Chencho despised Castro and communism and the way that countries like

Spain and Canada paid no heed to the embargo, how he loved sneaking into those salt baths—how he loved that one time when he'd seduced a young Spanish girl his age. He was caught in the act, fired on the spot, and forced to walk home through the tobacco crops with none of his clothing. It sounded terrible, but whenever Chencho would tell me the story, his eyes would water up, and he'd laugh so hard, he could barely make it to the end. Critical as Chencho was of Fidel Castro, he sure seemed to love his life in Cuba.

And it was the life Chencho might have lived had he stayed in Guanajay—a place on his uncle's field, rolling or gathering tobacco. Though he was around good Cuban food through his youth, it wasn't until he was exiled from his childhood home and sent to Miami that he appreciated it; he got a job at a Latin American cafeteria preparing puerco for the holidays and gained an interest in cooking: mincing, slicing, reducing, seasoning. Years of jumping from one cafeteria to the next made Chencho quite a prolific cook in Miami, so much so that he was recommended to me by the board, and so I commissioned him to work for the chamber based only on his amazing croquettes.

At the fundraiser I cohosted some days later, Chencho prepared a pig in the parking lot in a traditional Caja China. The meat of pigs roasted in Cajas Chinas slides off the bone—the flavor of the juice is proportionate to the crispiness of the skin—and at this fundraiser, when he saw those strips of meat pulling apart, he remarked that it reminded him of his uncle and his home in Cuba, all those brittle tobacco leaves loaded on pickup trucks in the mist of early morning to be sent into Havana for profit. He could still picture himself, wandering through the tobacco fields, leading stray girls onto the ground of the drying house. How he cherished recalling those romantic encounters.

"Chencho," I said, "what would your wife think? You talking about other girls?"

And Chencho laughed, serving me a plate of roast pork and yuca, adorned with the crispiest part of the ears. "I saved these for you, Albert. Don't tell my wife, por favor," he said. "Guanajay was a whole other world ago. That was a whole different me. Remember doesn't hurt anyone."

In This World of Ultraviolet Light

II

Today, I've been in Chencho's kitchen most of the day helping him prepare ropa vieja y frijoles negros and smoking cigars. I'm not sure this is how he planned on spending his evening, but here we are. It's not that I'm particularly good in the kitchen, but when I heard the news of Castro's stroke, I thought: *Is it time for Chencho's party?* I entered his office and asked him outright, and would you believe, he'd forgotten that he'd ever made an offer? He had other concerns too: the cost of such an event, the time and energy he'd have to spend planning, and, of course, the lack of time. "No, no, no," I said. "We're fixing this right now." In truth, I wasn't in the mood to work on budget plans—it being the end of the workweek and all. So, I sent everyone home early, feeling, in all earnestness, like Scrooge on Christmas morning.

Then, with Chencho by my side, I drove to Publix Super Market and purchased what he asked for, mainly, twenty pounds of flank and fifty tomatoes: "We will make the paste from scratch," he said. "It makes such a difference. You don't even know."

Chencho wasn't sure he had enough cumino in the house, so we stocked up on that too, along with bags of chicken bones and parts. "For the stock," he said. "You got to make it from scratch, or it's a waste." On the way out, while balancing this all in our arms and in the one cart with the wobbly wheel, Chencho said, "And we should get rum and coke, too, for us. Tonight, we drink to the promise of independence, and we prepare for tomorrow's feast. What do you say, my friend?"

"Hey," I said, "you don't think this is another false alarm, do you?"

"Mi amigo, Hugo Chavez flew to see him. Look around you. Mira!" So, I did, and all over the supermarket, there were others, seemingly preparing for a feast, all in the greatest of moods. "We are not alone in preparing for a party. This is no false alarm. The motherfucker is dead. It's over."

* * *

In his kitchen, there's a new iPod dock on his counter, playing Celia Cruz, and beside the dock, the mass of flank steaks, marbled and peeking through the ivory butcher paper. Glass bowls cover half of the kitchen island. Each needs to be filled: diced garlic, chopped parsley, ground cumino, stripped green bell peppers. Chencho hands me a navy apron emblazoned with palm trees, just like the one he's wearing, and he hands me a knife too. "Should we begin with the shirts or the pants?" he says, and he pokes my stomach with his elbow. "I'm just kidding, my friend. Hopefully, we won't have to use real clothes." Chencho reaches below the counter and pulls out a giant pressure cooker and sets it on the counter; it looks like a submarine with all those valves and airlocks. "Forty-two-quart capacity," he says. "Don't worry. This lid will not blow off the pot as long as we seal it correctly."

"Why ropa vieja?" I ask. "Is there some reason?"

"Well, it means old clothing. It's shredded meat cooked in a stew. The meat falls apart into a million little pieces: it's the most obvious choice for a new beginning, and look! I'll tell you why."

* * *

If you look online, you'll find that ropa vieja was born of the Caribbean migrations to and from the Canary Islands in Spain. And there are many variations throughout the Caribbean and South America, though Cubans regard it as one of their signature dishes. But, Chencho tells me, there's another story: the legend of Jose Luis of Oriente—a man so poor that he only owned a single outfit. Each day, Jose Luis would go out into the neighbor's garlic fields, trying to scrape by enough work so he could afford a meal. For many years, he was comfortable roaming Oriente's countryside in his tattered clothing. But then he fell in love with the neighbor's twelve-year-old daughter, Dunia—a tall girl for her age with long, black hair braided in ribbons. He often took his work breaks sitting under an old mango tree, watching Dunia play with her father's green parrot. And that parrot really loved her; it would follow her all around the yard, calling out to her, "Dunia, ven aquí. Dunia, baña te."

Using mostly lollipops and variations of flavored taffies, Jose Luis won Dunia's heart. And it wasn't long before Jose Luis decided to invite her family over so he could announce that they would be married. The trouble was the man was poor; he'd been working in the fields all day and had collected garlic and onions. But he could not afford the meat.

In This World of Ultraviolet Light

So, he took off his clothing and dumped it in a pot of boiling water; he'd been wearing that clothing for years. Dirt and sweat had baked into its fibers under the sun. It was the clothing he'd washed in the nearby river, downriver from the cattle farms—the one that sometimes ran with floating turds. Perhaps if this was any other man, the dish might have been ruined, but this man's love for Dunia was so strong that it turned the boiled clothing into a wonderful shredded-beef stew. That's what some people say, at least. Magic! Others think there was something about the clothing, being worn for so many years; it had become a sort of skin for Jose Luis and was therefore edible. But there are some who believe that Dunia's father shot Jose Luis—rightfully so—threw his body in the river, and later went home, where his own wife seasoned and boiled Jose Luis's clothing, which were later eaten to hide the evidence.

"If I was Dunia's father," Chencho says, relighting his cigar, "I would have shot Jose Luis too. I would have shot him in the cojones, and I would have boiled him, not his clothing!"

"But we can't be sure that's what happened."

"Por favor, Albert. She was a little girl—twelve years old. Jose Luis was shot. Who wouldn't shoot him and then eat his clothing? Or eat him? Or whatever, depending on the hunger."

"And what does this have to do with independence again?"

To this, Chencho gives me *the look* and says, "Weren't you just listening now?"

* * *

As Chencho seasons the flank, I turn to social media to craft an event page. Assuming fifty-plus attendees, I also book the same valet company that the chamber of commerce uses for special events. I'd hoped to book the Spam All-Stars for some entertainment, but it's too short of a notice, so I turn, instead, to a DJ I've worked with in the past. In addition to these logistics, there are obvious challenges in the kitchen. Making ropa vieja for this many people is no easy task. But Chencho can manage those challenges; years of experience catering large parties has made him economical and efficient in the kitchen, not to mention he has all the necessary equipment. But there are some less obvious issues that are specific to my role in the kitchen. For one thing, I am lousy with a knife, slicing my fingers now and then and bloodying up garlic cloves. Then there are the Cuba Libres, which Chencho keeps serving me. In truth, I'm too out of shape and clumsy to be prepping such a giant meal, but in the end, Chencho and his wife, Idania, help me finish so that each glass bowl is filled by nightfall. The only thing we have to keep checking on is the tomato pulp, which still has to reduce by quite a lot to become paste. But when it looks okay, Chencho scoops it out into the pressure cooker. All that is left is the cooking. And that's the beauty of pressure cookers. After we've loaded the pot with the meat, spices, and oils and then fill it halfway with chicken broth, we simply set it to cook and go out into the yard to sit by the pool and smoke more cigars.

Idania, a short, stocky woman with bangs falling over her large, dark eyes, follows us. She's sitting on the ledge of the pool, splashing her feet in the water by the floodlight when she says, "So he's dead. What's it to us? Sometimes I think we're not even Cuban anymore, living how we do."

Chencho undoes his apron and folds it beside him. "How could you say that, Idania?"

She pulls her feet out from the pool, wraps her arms around her knees, and turns to us. "We have iPhones, honey. We speak English more than Spanish. En el nombre de Dios, we're cooking enough food to feed a city. This is not Cuban. We are not like our brothers and sisters."

"If we're not Cuban, then who are we?" Chencho asks. "No somos Americano."

"Of course we are," she says. "We're American citizens."

"No. I know we are. You know what I mean."

His wife stands, wishes me a good night, and walks back toward the house. Standing by the French doors, she looks back and says, "So he's dead. What about it? The damage is done, no?"

She shuts the door and turns off the kitchen lights so that only the pool illuminates the yard. Chencho and I smoke more. But we don't talk. All I keep thinking about as I hold that cigar in my fingers is the pressure cooker. We'd sealed it, turned on the valves and levers just so. Chencho had even tested it. So, I'm not sure why I still fear that the lid will blow off in the middle of the night in some great explosion, covering his entire kitchen in pieces of shredded beef.

III

The day of the party, I meet with Chencho in advance of the event. It's October, and although the sun is near setting, the temperature is still in the lower nineties. I roll up my cuffs and shove a bottle of cold water in my jeans pocket. Chencho's wearing white linen pants and a yellow linen guayabera with a few cigars in his front pocket; he's walking along the pool's edge, lighting mosquito repellent tiki torches with a long match, as if those things have ever kept the bloodsuckers at bay.

"Did you see the news?" he asks.

"He's in a 'neurovegetative state,'" I say. "Not dead."

"Yes. Not dead, but he's all platanos in the brain. Enough reason to celebrate, no?"

"Chencho. You know me. I don't need a reason for good food."

On his lawn, between a few mango trees and stray cats, some men from the Fiesta Party Company are adding the finishing touches on a white tent they've raised, stringing red, white, and blue lights along the inner aluminum frame. By the tent, a young, platinum blond, large-breasted woman wipes down Chencho's outdoor bar, perfecting a display of scotch and rum bottles. Tables are being adorned with name tags and party favors—dulce de leche puffs inside small "que rico!" tasas—by Idania and a few kids: cousins and neighborhood friends. It's nice to see the youth.

The DJ sets up shop by the pool. "The music can bounce off the water, compadre. This is how Cubans work acoustics, my friend," Chencho says, patting my back, proudly, and motioning to the lights reflecting off his swimming pool. "We did it," he says, and I wonder whether he's referring to the party or to the fact that he's outlived the dictator of his nightmares. "We did it," he repeats.

"This is really lovely," I say. "Is there anything I can help you with?"

"Albert. Mingle. Go get me a scotch. Oh, and mingle. Please."

"But there's nobody here yet."

"Practice then," he says. "Because there will be people here. My people."

* * *

Later, I'm sitting at the bar, drinking a scotch and watching that cute blond fill her coolers with Presidente bottles and ice. Chencho's talking on his phone, pacing up and down alongside the pool.

"You watch baseball?" I ask. The bartender ignores me, so I ask, "What's your name?"

She's transferring beers from the cases to the cooler: "Qué?"

"Never mind," I say.

Despite their losing streak, Cubs' fans still march to Wrigley Field for each and every game, hoping for something different. Some critics believe it's the design of Wrigley Field that has doomed the Cubs. Low walls on the east side of the stadium allow Lake Michigan's gusts to sweep in, intensifying the challenges that come with pitching and batting. A few changes, these critics argue, could create a normal playing environment, which could lead to a victory. But Wrigley Field has been around for over a hundred years. It's an American landmark. It practically defines baseball. And nothing is going to change it, not critics, not science, only the will of God and some damn goat.

The blond pours a bucket of ice into the cooler and wipes her hands on her jean shorts. She takes a napkin, wipes her forehead, and says, "What brings you to this death-to-Fidel party?"

She's not as cute up close. Her hair's dyed. The roots are coming up just a bit where her hair is parted, and her face is pocked and smothered in concealer. But watching her sweating, serving me, her shirt tied up below her breasts, exposing her stomach, makes me want to take her out back and get to know her better, privately, in ways that would be completely inappropriate at the moment.

"I'm here for the food," I say. "And for my friend, Chencho."

"You asked me something earlier?"

"Yeah. If you watch baseball. And for your name."

"Of course. Cómo no," she says, kicking the cooler top shut. "I watch the Marlins. Diana."

In This World of Ultraviolet Light

"And the Cubs?" I ask. "I'm Albert, by the way."

"No. They suck. The Cubs, I mean. Not you."

"I watch them!"

"The Cubs? Well, then you should stop," she says and laughs.

"If you were from Chicago, the North Side, you'd watch them."

"Maybe," she says, returning to the beer cases. "But who'd want to live in Chicago?"

"Really?"

"Um . . . yeah. Chi-*cago*. Like *cágate en tu madre*. You get it?" Then she returns to her work.

I laugh, even if I feel offended. I could imagine myself in Cuba, taking Diana into Chencho's uncle's drying house and loving her under the drying tobacco leaves—two prisoners exiled to paradise, perfectly content simmering around so much hunger and splendor. But there I go again, overromanticizing what it's like to be Cuban. Maybe if I'd been born in Cuba, in Guanajay, maybe I would have braved the sharks and currents of the Florida Straits too. Or maybe not. I don't know; I could be tremendo comunista with a woman like Diana in my arms. Why think of Castro at all?

* * *

When the guests begin to arrive, the party functions like the perfectly oiled machine that it is. Guests turn their keys into the valet staff that I've hired. Even under the heat, they're dressed for the occasion: men in wool suits or button-up shirts and ties; women in knee-length cocktail dresses. It's like a funeral, but festive. They strut along a dimly lit path around the side of Chencho's house, toward the sounds of trumpets and drums and all the magic of our DJ illuminating his backyard.

As a point, Chencho takes me around the party—helping himself to butler-served ham croquettes or tostones along the way—while introducing me to his friends as his aplantado boss at the Doral Chamber of Commerce. And he always says this: "Now why don't you tell my American friend why we should all be celebrating Castro's death." Answers vary: the appropriation of land, the imprisonment of loved ones, betrayal, poverty, hunger, the abandonment of the Cuban people—how

Castro had taken the jewel of the Caribbean and allowed it to crumble. But these reasons seem rehearsed. Perhaps there was a time, long ago, when these Miami Cubans had felt pain and loss at their separation from their homeland, but on this night, while drinking premium rum in Chencho's yard, the celebration seems more like an act of vengeance. For the most part, the first generation of Cubans had prospered outside their home country; they'd built Miami, turning it into the metropolis it is today. They'd raised families, had children, and become grandparents. And how appropriate now, I think, that they look back on all their success, forsaking the man who had forever transformed their lives by leading them into exile. Who would they be without Castro?

* * *

Chencho arranges it so that I sit with his cousins, all of whom also grew up on his uncle's tobacco farm. Dinner is plated; a slop of ropa vieja on a small rectangular mold of white rice. Beside the rice are four fried plantains and a small white bowl of black beans. Written in sweet chili sauce along the ridge of the plate is tonight's theme: "Cuba Libre!!!" The presentation is everything I'd hoped for.

At the center of the tent there's a white cake with the island of Cuba detailed in green icing and beside this cake, a table with a pyramid of plastic champagne flutes. Chencho says a few words: "May that rotten son of a bitch forever rot in hell. And may we one day return to our homeland, freely." And then with the help of Idania, they pour the champagne into the highest plastic flute. Champagne bubbles up at the top and flows from one tier of flutes to the next. Everybody stands, applauds. I set my napkin on my chair and go out to the front to smoke a cigarette. The valet drivers I hired are there, sitting on the sidewalk, listening to the radio and playing a game of dominos.

I sit beside them to watch. "Do you mind?" I ask.

They seem guarded with me there, but after a few domino hands, they loosen up. One of them offers me some chiviricos—fried and sugared dough. "Qué haces aquí? What you doing with us, boss?"

Another one of them remarks, pointing back toward the party, "You should be having fun."

"Just needed some fresh air," I say.

"You should go to Cuba," one of the valets says. "So much fresh air. Not like this country. Work. Work. Work. For what? Walmart?" Perhaps sensing he has spoken out of turn, he adds, "But, you know, I'm grateful to be in America. It's just, I thought it would be different. Not like this."

"Well," I say, "I don't know if I'd call this America. It's just Miami. You should see Chicago. America's Second City. Beautiful in the springtime. And Wrigley Field. There's no place like it."

"Maybe I will," one of the drivers says. "And maybe you'll see Cuba. Let's make it so." And with that, we shook, and though I knew there was nothing binding to it, I thought, I should *really* go.

* * *

At the end of the night, I finally eat my food, and then I sit with Chencho in his living room watching television while the party service company cleans up the back. He's had a great time; he's always wanted to celebrate the death of Castro. "Only one problem," he says, flipping the channel to the Spanish news. A reporter is walking with Castro alongside a tobacco field, asking him about his health. Castro looks sick, but he's wearing a black tracksuit, new; Castro smiles and says that he's better than ever. He holds up the previous day's newspaper, just to prove it, and he laughs.

"A foolish man holding onto a childish revolution," Chencho says, kicking off his shoes and socks. "That man will never die."

"Why think about him then?" I ask. "If he bothers you so much, why think of him?"

"You still don't see what I'm telling you, my friend?"

"I'm just asking you a question."

"You're telling me to forget what he did. I won't! Don't you understand that?"

"Look! The Cubs have had it bad," I say, "but it doesn't ruin me. They'll have their chance."

"The Cubs? What the fuck do the Cubs have to do with this?"

"I think there's a lot in common."

"He liked baseball too. Fidel Castro," Chencho says, sitting up in his chair, lighting a cigar.

Chencho smokes and rocks in his chair, clearly upset by what I've said. He closes his eyes, and I want to cheer him up. He can be so difficult. I imagine that his mind's going back to his home in Guanajay. I imagine Chencho as a little boy, covered in dirt, sneaking into the drying house to chew leaves. It must have been an idyllic childhood, but now that's gone: his home, his chores, his rags. Replaced by a lovely home and wife in Miami. Replaced by a job in the culinary arts. Replaced by wool suits and Italian leather shoes. Replaced by English and capitalism and independence and traffic and all the things that make us American. All that remains of his childhood now is the smoke—tobacco leaves packed and rolled so many years ago—so I bum a cigar and smoke too. And we smoke until we can no longer see each other even though we're sitting in the same room.

3

Never through Miami

His first time in Miami International Airport, Palacio was dazzled. How do I know? Coño! Because that's how I felt when I arrived an eternity ago. I was eighteen and standing in this long terminal of waiting and canceled flights and indecipherable announcements and food—oh God, food!—the whole corridor fragrant with frying oil, salt, so much grease I felt full just breathing. Back then, it was easy for me to break my visa and seek asylum. My parents were already dead—or at least those Castro sympathizers were dead to me. I arrived in 1993, the peak of the special period. For God's sake, the pretzels I'd been given on the plane were the most nutritious thing I'd eaten in three days.

Enough about me. Palacio! He was a different kind of Cuban altogether. Immigration officers in Havana's José Martí Airport must have been completely befuddled by him. Imagine being a fly on the wall in that interrogation room and seeing those officers' faces when Palacio answered, "Why are you traveling to the US?" with "Amor, man! Love. I'm going to visit mi jeva, hermano."

If I'd said something like that when I got here twenty-five years ago, the officers would have dragged me to a windowless room and beat the shit out of me. Even in 2018, during Palacio's journey, it was a miracle the officers let him leave the island. They must have recognized something dumb or true in Palacio, but he must have perplexed them nonetheless. Because he could afford airfare. He was a black tour guide and liaison for American tourist companies—a steward for Obama-era policy. He was an anomaly: a Cuban under the Revolution, earning a living wage—an Afro-Cuban with mobility and access and with no desire whatsoever to leave his family or his beloved country for the capitalismo of the United States. I didn't know young people like Palacio existed, who'd opt to stay in Cuba, to build a life there shuttling the wealthy from site to site.

How he must have looked forward to that week in LA. What would he do? I don't know. Some people believed he was going to propose to his girl—sweep her off her feet and bring her back to the island. But Palacio was too suave for that. I thought he was going to spend the entirety of his vacation in his girl's bungalow, lying naked under the AC, feeling the cold on their sweat. Afterward, they'd walk to McDonald's, share fries, eat a Quarter Pounder each—consume enough calories to ravage each other again. I could live a lifetime like that. Because when you love someone, you don't need much. You don't even need the person to love you back. Everything in the world is an extension of your lover: the ginormous and lush cosmetic ads affixed to the airport walls, the colorful vending machines, interfaces blinking, beckoning you to reach out and buy something. I know this feeling because that's how I still feel toward Madely today, even if we've long split up, even if she is a criminal, even if I am in some new relationship—some glorified prison cell.

Palacio—when he arrived, he must have been elated. On tape, he seemed like a speck of glee fluttering about the arrivals, happy to be in circulation, his only thought: to make his connection. He was anyone, no one, flaunting his mobility and confidence. Then, what can I say? He approached our Delta help desk in Concourse A and met my ex, Madely, and this is where our worlds converged.

* * *

I met Madely at Delta. We went through customer service training together in '99. I remember that I instantly disliked her hair—cherry red, frazzled, curly, and spilling onto her shoulders—it was too loud for me, too much for 8:00 a.m. in some moldy office building. She wore something smelling of vanilla and musk, and she'd sit next to me so that I'd have to inhale her all day—an invasive scent that made me feel like someone had flayed me entirely and replaced my skin with polyester. We never really touched except when she'd put her hand on my thigh to get my attention, and I'd put my hand on hers, peel her fingers off, and whisper, "Coño, Madely. Qué's eso? I'm trying to pay attention."

While our instructor led class, she'd lean into me and whisper nothings: how bored she was, if she could see my notes. And she'd criticize Delta's customer service approach—always in a Spanish that was reffier and more exaggerated than I felt comfortable with. There I was, studying like my life depended on it, and Madely didn't raise her pencil once. She sat back, acting like the job didn't matter, trying only to set up a date with me. Or she'd see me writing vigorously, and she'd pull the pencil out of my hand and say, "Easy there, compadre." Because that's another thing. This woman, who'd left Cuba and her parents at just seven years old, who hated Cuba and who spoke English very well, who was raised in the US by her late uncle, yes, this woman acted like she was the most Cuban fucking spokesperson on the planet. And you know what? I think she might have been.

When it came time to take our final exam—when we each had to sit up front with the instructor and take turns demonstrating our customer service skills to an actress, a mean old white lady intent on ruining our day—it was Madely who outshone us all. I'll never forget; the actress slapped the table, yelled, "I paid nine hundred dollars! For this ticket! And you're telling me! My flight has been canceled!" With each pause in her statement, she'd slap the table again. It was brutal to watch.

Madely didn't even attempt the script. She simply sat up and said, "Mira, chica! You think it's okay to yell at people? My uncle who raised me, God bless his soul, he never yelled at me, and what gives you the right? What'd I do to you, huh? Cálmate, coño, y help me help you, gringa."

The actress was dumbfounded. Maybe it's because she didn't speak Spanish. Who knows? She'd probably seen Madely—that frazzled hair and those wild hoop earrings—and she'd made some kind of judgment, like it was okay to talk to her that way. As if she were an animal or something. The actress sat down, smiled wide, almost embarrassed, and said, "You're right. I'm sorry. You're so damn convincing! Isn't she great, everyone? Let's give her a round of applause. Madely, right? Madely, the natural persuader. This is going places. You all hear that. Learn from her while you can."

After training, I didn't really hang out with Madely again. That's how it is sometimes—it takes years for you to realize who the most important person in your life is. We worked different corners of that massive airport, so when we did run into one another, it was in passing. We were busy people. Life moved on. Then in 2011, I was promoted to manager, and, just like that, I was thrust back into Madely's life. You see, I was assigned to Concourse A—her turf. It was I, in the end, who had climbed the corporate ladder. Madely was my subordinate, and I felt underqualified.

It's no secret. Despite her reputation, I didn't think much of her abilities or her work ethic. She'd bypass rules or pretend that certain policies didn't apply to her. Here was this woman who thought she was above protocol, a woman who I'd seen blow up on customers who, sure, deserved it—so many of them do. But I feared that she'd let me have it one day too, and the last thing I wanted was Madely, Category 5, barreling down on me. It was clear. I couldn't manage her.

This is all to say that I did the best I could to stay out of Madely's way when she was on the warpath, to be distant, to put my hand on hers and peel her fingers off when she'd grab my thigh and apply pressure.

Then, about five years ago, I was helping my tía-abuela, Nana, pick up essentials at Publix, and who did we run into, strutting in her Delta

In This World of Ultraviolet Light

uniform like she was the fucking Gestapo, out for an errand? Madely, thick, voluptuous, filled out in ways that made it uncomfortable to be around her—hair just as cherry red and crazy as the day I met her. I swear, we were right next to the produce section, so far removed from her location, and even then, I thought I smelled that vanilla musk. It was unbearable how much Madely got under my skin—Madely, holding a can of frijoles and reading the nutrition label like she really cared about the sodium levels or the sugar, nails long, pink.

Seeing her far off, I panicked and backed up. I turned the cart around, but poor Nana; she was so confused by my erratic movements. We were dancing, us and the cart, and when I'd finally directed us to an escape, just past the stacked melons, Nana, dazed by our twirling, tripped.

The way she fell, it reminded me of the first time I went to IHOP, and I was trying to pour that thick pancake syrup out, but the liquid just wouldn't drop. I didn't act as fast as I should have. I just watched, incredulous and a little distracted. It was Madely who dropped her can of frijoles and ran over like some Super Mujer, some new Latina Marvel Comics character, and caught her. What can I say? She's good at what she does—the protector, the fist. But that didn't mean Nana needed to invite her over for dinner, nudging me the whole time as if to say, *Mira, Xavier, she's tremendo mujer. Don't be a pendejo. Ask her out. Give me bisnietos.*

And I have to admit that when she came over for dinner, I despised her still, her vanilla musk especially, until some drinks later. Nana left us out on the lanai, and I started getting this feeling, this, I don't know, and Madely lifted her shirt, just beside her belly button, revealing her pudgy softness, her happy trail. She took my hand, my fingers, and led me to a scar, a little smile. It was beautiful, that cut. "What happened there?"

"Ectopic pregnancy," she said. "I was once a mother."

With those words, she kissed my neck and fondled my breast through my shirt like I was the chick. It was nice when she took control, made me feel like a thing she could put her nails into. Because I could go limp, relax. I could swirl that strange word around in my mouth, *ectopic*, and feel, for a moment, warm and lodged against her and forgetful of any resistance I'd ever harbored for her.

*   *   *

On March 4, 2019, Detective Laura Machado found me in Concourse A. It was one of those loud oppressive days at MIA. Storms along the East Coast had crippled the sky, causing delays and cancellations. But what really matters—and what you must understand at this point—is that Madely and I had broken up. To say we'd broken up is a little disingenuous. We'd never officially been together. Everything after that night at Nana's had been so casual, yet it still felt like I'd been dumped, badly, and there I was, back at work, expected to still function normally as her supervisor, expected not to take note or become jealous of her fleeting love interests. Let's just say, I didn't handle this new phase in our relationship well. Something had happened. A flashpoint. I might have yelled at her in front of everyone or even called her a dirty slut in front of a customer. All week, I'd been expecting a call from corporate. I couldn't sleep because I thought I was going to lose my job.

This is why when I noticed a woman in a suit watching me, I was afraid that Madely had revealed the scope of our relationship to headquarters. I was convinced this woman was there to fire me. She was so casual looking, leaning against a supersized wall banner advertising the Florida Keys—a picture of a pristine beach and a lone bikini top soaking in the surf. She wore a tight black suit, dark pantyhose, dark pumps. She was gorgeous, like an even more feminine Leonardo DiCaprio from his *Titanic* days, only less blond, less pale, with longer hair and pencil-thin lips. From my vantage point, across the concourse, it seemed as though she was studying me, notepad in hand.

I sidled up beside my subordinates, all deep in the throes of their customer service arguments, and whispered, "Have you seen that woman before? Is she corporate?" Nobody knew. I was so concerned by this woman's presence that even customers began to take note—all those customers standing in line, without seats on planes, displaced and miles from home, all looking over their shoulders, trying to figure out who was making me so nervous. And when some lady in a wheelchair made a beeline for our desk, a small portable kennel in her hands—probably another dead pet or service animal, claimed by an overhead bin—I thought I'd lost my job for sure. But this woman didn't care about our daily operations. She hardly hesitated when the customer pulled a stiff kitten out from the kennel. I know because that was the moment she approached me, flashed her badge, and rescued me from my work. She introduced herself as a detective for Miami and asked if she could take a look at our surveillance footage, specifically, the tapes for the morning of September 11, 2008. She'd said something about a roster, though in my nervousness, I'd heard "restroom," so I led her to the public bathroom—the one right by the Starbucks. She was confused, but went along anyway. I can only imagine what she expected to find as she turned the tiled corner.

"In here?" she asked.

"Yes. In there."

Well, it didn't take her long to realize there were no surveillance tapes in the women's restroom. When she came out, she was annoyed, through she'd clearly taken the opportunity to freshen up. She pulled out a warrant and everything. I apologized for the miscommunication and complied with her request, of course. Rather than manning the customer service desk, I, gladly, stepped away and spent the better part of a day watching those tapes with the detective. I was her little helper—an expert, praised for my ability to offer necessary background and context.

Madely was in the footage. When she'd look at the camera, I'd get this feeling—like she was the one watching us. At precisely 10:37 a.m. on the tapes, I observed some black dude take his place in the customer service line, roller bag in tow. "There. That's him! Palacio!" the detective said, reaching for nothing on the table, her motion suggesting she might have expected a bowl of popcorn. She elbowed me in the gut, laughed. "Sorry. What can you tell me about this guy?"

Palacio looked like someone used to making a line, and I would know from my days collecting my parents' rations in Havana. God! Americans don't know what it is, really, to make a line. There were other indications that he was Cubano. He wore dark-blue jeans, a white polo, collar up, but all in a style that we hadn't seen in the US in over a decade. He sported an afro, taped up, soup-bowl style. He had excellent posture, and when he glanced back (at what, I don't know), I saw his face—un papi chulo, with full lips, supple. He had chiseled features, and he was scruffy in ways that all those young Miami Cuban Americans haven't learned to embrace. I was jealous. This young and attractive man was so engaged with Madely, so wound up in conversation, that I turned to the detective myself, and I thought to ask, *And how about you? What can you tell me?* But I didn't.

"Well?" the detective asked.

In the footage, he gestured to his ticket, and I knew he was asking about his gate. It had been changed, and he was certainly lost. Then it happened. He pulled out his Cuban passport and handed it to Madely. They leaned into one another, exchanged whispers. I wish we had the audio!

Madely had no reason to ask for a customer's passport. She wasn't an immigration officer or a boarding agent. "What is she doing?" I asked. Then, as if this were occurring in real time, and as if Madely knew that I was watching her, she slipped his passport into her bra, that blue Cuban booklet snuggled up against her breast in ways she'd never let me. Palacio looked like he might reach into her shirt to retrieve it, but he hesitated. Of course he did. And that's when Madely took his hand and walked him off the frame.

"Wait! What?" I shouted.

"Palacio Osha Hernan has been missing for about a month."

"Missing? How so?"

"This video makes the woman a prime suspect in his abduction."

"No," I said. "Madely? Yeah, right."

"What is Madely's last name?"

"Sanchez."

"Did she work the remainder of that shift?"

I checked my records. On the day in question, she'd clocked out early. I didn't remember approving that. I thought, *Slut! What a bitch! Cunt! Whore! Fucking a perfect stranger!* I was so angry, I wanted to call her right then and there and let her have it.

"Xavier," said Machado. "Calm down. Can you give me her schedule this week? Her address? Her phone number?"

I wrote this all down on the back of my business card and handed it to the detective.

Machado thanked me, kissed my cheek. I know. I know. This seems odd, but it isn't entirely uncustomary in a place like Miami. I didn't think much of it. Or later, when before leaving, Machado turned and asked, "You're not going to tell her we're onto her, are you?" The way she said it, I felt like she knew that I had shared something deep and private with Madely. Detectives, I imagined, could sense such things. Somewhere in our conversation, I had betrayed myself. I knew it.

"Why do you think I'd do that? Do I seem like that kind of person?"

"I don't know you," she said. "But don't." And she ran off, phone already in hand.

Are you surprised, then, that I texted Madely immediately? *Don't come into work!! Police!*

The least Madely could have done was respond with a mere *Thanks! :)*

No. Madely didn't even do that. Didn't even respond when I texted, *New boy toy, huh?*

* * *

Why had Madely seduced him? I've had to create my own theories. I think she must have detected something in his Spanish—a dialect picked apart by a life in Regla, a decade collaborating with the celebrated hip-hop trio Protagonismo (not that he contributed to the songwriting. No. Palacio was all for show, the sexy one, shirtless, slick, obsidian, dancing in the background, the bulge in his shorts swaying, swelling to inhuman proportions. Of course Madely took an interest in him). His speech must have sounded familiar but not, Cuban but in a register embargoed by time and place, ajiacoed in a pressure cooker in the Afro-Cuban community overlooking Havana and its bay—the same community that Madely's own family hailed from. I think she wanted to save him because she'd lost so much: not just the promise of motherhood, but her parents, her uncle, and me.

People who don't live in Miami don't understand the Cuban fervor in the metropolis by the sea—the way those Cubans can be so righteous, brimming with the desire and intensity to save every last marielito from Castrolandia. Madely must have seen Palacio's passport, and she must have assumed he needed asylum, required it even if he insisted otherwise. She must have thought herself a martyr, offering up the kingdom of her body for his salvation. And Palacio, how could he not be attracted to Madely? Who wouldn't wink (wink wink) and follow her out of the airport?

Mira. I know Madely, like, really good. I get it. We didn't really date, not in any traditional sense. We were something beyond a relationship, and always in her clean-smelling home near Kendall, and me, learning things about myself, things I wouldn't have admitted to anyone a few years ago. Like the submissive impulses I'd get when I was near her. There. I said it.

Put me and Madely in the same room, and it's like a switch goes off. I don't know. It's this hunger I get to be used, directed, draped over the side of the bed, and, well, I'm probably oversharing. But I don't care. All my life, I didn't get it. Why people wanted things in there. It's a one-way tunnel, I thought, part of the digestive system, opposite the mouth for a reason.

But Madely taught me that I didn't really know myself, never really had. Just trust me when I say I know her really good now—Madely and all her patriotism, a woman who can be so gung ho and ravenous. Sure. But some nights, warm beneath the heavy comforter, she'd talk and talk, and though I couldn't stand the way she spoke Spanish, I'd listen and absorb every one of her secrets.

* * *

Long before I'd become intimate with her, Madely managed to bring her mother and father to Miami. It had been quite an endeavor securing their visas, signing over assets in order to claim them. How distraught she became when her family didn't even last three months in Miami; they hated it. Miami had been too much—too much work, too much food, too many expenses. Apparently, her family preferred the Cuban devil to the American one, but Madely couldn't reconcile what was an obvious betrayal. To her, they were no better than the lazy, bad Cubans on the island. They were leeches who'd come and taken her for everything she had. They'd left and gone to hell, as far as she told me. She was so mad. Those nights when she'd get worked up about family, it was sad to hear her villainize them comparing them to Fidel; it was sad to hear it in her voice—tears—though she never actually cried. I told her once, "Why not call them?" She bit my neck so hard, I thought she ripped a piece of me off. And you know what? It felt good to be bit, even if it really scared me too.

Sometimes I'd touch her, rub her, and climb atop as if to make love, and she'd push me off. She never explicitly told me why she'd act this way. I suspected it had to do with the trauma of her pregnancy. How losing the promise of her child must have devastated her. I tried to do everything that I could to help Madely cope with her grief, but the only thing that ever helped and the only thing she wanted was my bottom against her, so I let her feel her fingers into me, let her press her sadness into me until it spread and blossomed into something else. Her fervor, the way she'd dig her nails into my hips, tigerlike, I always wondered how she'd ever allowed her family to slip through her claws in the first place. I couldn't imagine Madely allowing anyone to escape her life. Her depth was a mystery to me. Her home was a mystery. She'd locked off certain rooms: her kid's nursery; the room her parents had stayed in during their short visit to the US. When we were seeing one another, she'd explicitly forbidden me from entering either of those rooms. The rooms were off-limits, and it was weird, but I dealt with the rule at first. If Madely needed those sealed rooms to cope, then I was okay respecting that. Even in our lovemaking, if she didn't like the idea of me penetrating her, then I was okay with that too. I say this because I want to be clear: this was the kind of lover Madely was, somebody that could hold on to you for all your life, even long after you'd parted with her. Someone who could enshrine you. And maybe if I hadn't peeked into those rooms of hers, we'd still be together now. Maybe I'd have my own little room that people wouldn't be allowed into.

* * *

Just hours after I met Detective Machado, when I was rinsing out my Tupperware in the break room, the news broke that Palacio had been found. I couldn't believe it. A newly minted free man, and Palacio was already sitting across from Channel 7's Belkys Nerey, nothing at all sparkly like the man I'd seen earlier in the footage. It was strange for time to collapse that way for me. I'd only just learned of the man—had seen him young in the tapes—only to see him hours later, aged, worn, as though he'd been lost at sea for months. Actually, he looked worse than even the freshest balseros.

The news report cut to footage from Palacio's hospital stay, and who was at his side? Detective Machado, glamorous as ever, hair down, blouse semi-unbuttoned. "Our prime suspect," she said, "is still on the loose. Her name is Madely Sanchez. If you know . . ."

There I was at MIA, watching all this news unfold, watching the detective speak when I got a text from Machado herself: *Call me. It's urgent. I have to talk to you :)*. It seemed like an act of sorcery in the moment, seeing the detective in two places, until I realized the footage was previously recorded. I wondered, what did the detective want with me now? So I didn't call right away. I wanted to think things through, to make sure she hadn't figured out that I'd texted Madely when I shouldn't have.

*　*　*

I did call Machado, of course, and the following night we met for dinner at the Rusty Pelican. We sat outdoors overlooking downtown. I was in my Delta uniform (because I always have to work), nervous. I felt like a criminal—I was a criminal—wholly underdressed for the occasion, especially sitting across from the detective, who wore a stunning gold-sequin dress and matching earrings.

"You can relax, sidekick," she said and winked. "Please. Let's enjoy ourselves."

"You don't look like a detective tonight," I said.

She smiled, licked her lips. "Tonight," she said, "we celebrate."

"You said it was urgent?"

"All celebrations are," she said, raising her hand for our server, who brought us a bottle of champagne.

"On me," the detective said, and we toasted to Palacio's safety.

"With all due respect," I said, "what is this really?"

"I don't know."

The detective ordered the strip. I ordered fish and chips.

We ate in silence, listening to the breeze in the palm fronds. Because we didn't talk about the case, we stared at one another, then at the city, and then at one another again, awkwardly, until all at once, we finished the bottle, closed out the tab, and ambled over to the parking lot. At this point, I think we were both a little wobbly from the champagne. She pinched by butt and laughed.

I said, "Detective!"

"Yes?"

It was unsaid, really, but I knew our attraction was mutual. When she put her hand on my waist, I put mine on hers, peeled back her fingers, said, "No."

She laughed at me and said, "I need an upgrade, please."

And I made some unfortunate joke about reward points.

Weaving in and out of parked luxury cars, the detective pushed me up against a light post and kissed me. It rained moths; we were in a storm of them. She led me to her car—a white roadster—and she opened the passenger door, invited me inside. Then she entered the driver's side, revved up the car so that the AC was blowing in our faces. The whole moment was wonderfully gluttonous and excessive, especially with the entire city erect behind her. It reminded me of the first time I'd come to the US—how everything seemed so shiny and so utterly real.

She kissed me again. Look. I'd known the detective was romantically interested in me. The moment she nudged me when we were watching the tapes, I felt it. And when you're a guy like me, approaching middle age, you don't question when these opportunities present themselves.

Can I say, any other moment in my life, kissing her all night would have been something to truly celebrate. But Madely had changed me in some radical ways. Don't get me wrong, Detective Machado was a beautiful woman, but being with her felt wrong and scandalous, like I'd stepped over some line I'd never meant to cross. I'd been so open with Madely for so long. She'd peeled back parts of my sexuality I didn't even know were there.

* * *

Palacio was moneyless, still "vacationing" in the US with an expiring visa, and at the mercy of other people's GoFundMes. What made him stay? It's hard to say. He seemed so caught up in the hysteria, in being led from interview to interview, constantly pushed to revisit his abduction—to live as if the only real thing in his life was the time he spent abducted by Madely—that he became angry, quick to demonize all of the US. This was a bad look for him, and I didn't think he was being fair with his time in the US or about his time with Madely. I mean, it wasn't the United States that abducted him; government officials, to the contrary, had helped him. And as for Madely, sure, she'd done something reprehensible, and she would have to answer for her crimes, but she was a person too, and it angered me to see her (or anything, for that matter) reduced to two-second sound bites.

Worse was when the media caught up with Palacio's ex-girlfriend. I was at the detective's house, and it was late; she was already asleep, her head on my lap. I was dozing off myself when that dramatic news music came on—the one Channel 7 had made especially for stories about Palacio. It was an exclusive with Marcela Diaz—Palacio's ex—all done up on the screen like she was auditioning for a role. She said, "If he really loved me, he wouldn't have walked off with that insane woman . . . he clearly was unfaithful . . . all Cubans are that way . . . I'm glad she made him suffer."

When asked if she'd communicated with him, she responded, "I'll never talk to that motherf—er again." Yet as she said that, she teared up. She didn't say much after, but it was clear Palacio had broken her heart. But would you know, a few months later, it gets announced that Marcela would be the new *Bachelorette*. Palacio may be back in Cuba by now, but her career is still going strong, as strong as some D-list actress's could be.

It was all such a spectacle, especially the day Madely was last seen. Again, this was all broadcast live. Police officers stormed Tropical Park, surrounded Madely at the batting cages. She'd been practicing her swing. If you watch the clip carefully, as I have, you'll see that Machado was there too. In fact, when Madely swung at the arresting officer, then got tased and dropped on her back, you'll see that it was Detective Machado who'd done the tasing—no hesitation.

If there's one thing I've learned about Madely, though, it's that things always get more complicated around her. You see, Madely escaped. How? I wish I knew. All we have is the footage. Somehow, Madely got out of the cuffs, climbed out of the police car, and bounded out, heading back into Tropical Park. Detective Machado chased her over the large hill at the park's heart, but when she made it to the top, Madely had vanished, truly. No matter where the police looked, she didn't turn up, and, as you can imagine, this miraculous vanishing act intrigued the media even more. Everyone, from the lady at the cafeteria to the goddamned orange-haired false president of ours, had an opinion. For some, Madely was a patriot, a warrior of capitalism, a scourge on Castro's legacy; to others, she was a lunatic, taking advantage of someone with little security in the US. Late-night talk shows had segments on her: *Where in the World Is Madely Sanchez?* and *The Madely Files*. Anchors on Fox News suggested that Madely had not acted alone; rather, many Latinas across the country would soon emulate her—more of a reason to build a wall and keep those lousy no-good criminals out.

The detective had to make a public announcement assuring everyone that Madely would be found. By this point, there were all kinds of government agencies involved, but the detective remained on the case nonetheless. She was determined, confident, trusted. In bed, it was another story. "Tell me! How did she do it? Are you going to tell me, you fucking liar?"

She was convinced that my reluctance to speculate indicated that I was hiding something from her too, and what was I to do? I most certainly was hiding something. The way the detective prodded me, it was as if she'd always known that me and Madely had been intimate during one part of my life, even if I'd neglected to mention it. I suspect that she knew that I fantasized about Madely when I was with her in bed. "Fantasize" is the wrong word. I longed for her; I grieved for Madely so much. She was over the top, sure; she'd always been, but I knew her. I really knew her, and it saddened me knowing what she'd come to—a criminal on the run. One night, we were in bed, restless. I leaned into the detective, kissed her cheek, and tasted her tears. This confused me. "Why are you crying?" I asked. The detective didn't answer. She shoved me and gave me her back.

* * *

When I started looking for Madely, I wasn't sure if I was doing it for myself or for the detective. How I did it? I studied those damn newsreels. I tried to learn as much as I possibly could about Palacio. Through Belkys's interviews, I learned he'd been held captive in one of Madely's bedrooms, leather collar around his neck, chained like a dog to the iron bars on the window, wrists bound together. Coño, Palacio. How honest he was, unafraid of how people would see him or think of him. I envied that about him. Every little dirty detail, he shared; it was impressive. All of it.

For instance, each morning, Madely would unlock his bedroom door and enter, wrapped in an American flag. She'd recite the Pledge of Allegiance, sliding the flag off slowly, teasing him, violating him. It was all so juicy, and rather than shun him for his confessions, the world was fascinated. Nobody mocked him. Nobody made him feel like less of a person. I didn't expect that. They loved him when he made his suffering public; they hated him when he spoke with reason (like that time Belkys asked why he was still in the US if he was already free to go home, and he responded "Because some can't go home," and he proceeded to discuss Central American asylum seekers, Haitians in detention centers). Who wanted to tune in to something so didactic?

And let me just share this inconvenient truth: Madely is gorgeous when she's all dommed up. God! There's Palacio on screen describing these incidents, and all I see is Madely, red curly hair, shoulder length, bronzed skin, leather knee-high boots, leather studded bra, leather fittings for her strap-on, lifelike, and veins like tributaries, hardened, the taste of rubber and silicone. I'd get hard just thinking about it, the way she'd make me kneel before her, and how she'd hold my head with both hands and thrust or make me bite it, or how she'd push my chin up just so and slap my face with it, tell me to keep my mouth shut, slapping harder when I'd open to taste. It's exciting just to confess to this all—to say things aloud that I always thought would be forever buried inside me.

Of course, Palacio didn't mention his appetites, but I could see them in his eyes, the way he'd look away from Belkys when she was speaking, like he was elsewhere, back in Madely's home and learning to be submissive and learning to love America, the national anthem blaring, and Madely wearing our flag like a cape, thrusting freedom,

In This World of Ultraviolet Light

jubilation, and all her inalienable rights into his body. And when Belkys asked this one shitty question—"But was she really violating you if you were aroused?"—Palacio cried right there on live television, unsure himself, and viewers loved it all.

I know! Six months of this. Can you imagine?

He admitted, toward the end, he would have swallowed anything—orange-face man, Islamophobia, white supremacy. Everything Madely said tasted rich and salty, good on the way down, but empty, so empty that he was always hungry, always malnourished, and hearing him talk about her made me wonder whether I, too, had been starving myself during my time with Madely.

* * *

Palacio was destined to die in exile in Madely's home, but he got lucky, or he was persistent, or both. Per his own accounts, the first time he tried to escape, he had spent weeks leading her to believe he was content with his bondage and imprisonment. He wanted Madely to believe that he was a convert, that he'd become a Cuba-hating Cuban. This, according to Palacio, pleased her. It's likely the reason why, one day, Madely eased his restraints, removed the chain affixed to his leather collar, and said, "Don't make me regret this, you got it?" She left for work, and during that brief shift, Palacio dug through the ceiling with a hanger, which he'd folded over again and again until it could easily claw through drywall. When he'd made a large enough hole, he pulled his body into the attic crawl space above his room, only to discover that the crawl space was sectioned off by steel mesh grates. Coño. It still chills me to think of all the lengths Madely took to contain him. Surely, she hadn't fortified that room for him alone. What would inspire her, really, to do such a thing?

In any case, when she got home, Big Mac meal in her hand, and saw all the mess he'd made, she tossed his food in the garbage and said, as an act of punishment, that he could eat the drywall like the ungrateful desgraciado that he was. She locked him up for three days. He didn't eat the drywall, not raw, not without boiling it. "What kind of Cuban did she think I was?" he told Belkys, smiling, though I could see past his smile. Of course he'd eaten it. He'd at least tasted it.

There was another instance. After "el sexo"—a phrase that Palacio used, but which made him cringe—she'd fallen asleep at his side, the loop of keys affixed to the clasp on her strap-on. Palacio carefully removed the keys, freed himself, and ran out of the house. But she must have heard the beeping from her home security system—the door ajar—because she ran out too, got in her car, and nearly ran him down. Actually, she did clip him, just a touch. Then she coerced him into her home.

After that, Madely was always careful around him. Palacio lost hope for months. Then, one afternoon, as she was securing his restraints, Madely received a text message and departed frantically. Palacio didn't know what had spooked her, and he didn't know how long she'd be gone, but he took the opportunity to try for another escape. This time, he tugged at his collar, and to his astonishment, it came undone. He slipped his head out and cautiously made his way to the front door, which was secured with an iron gate. So were all the windows in the house. That didn't stop him, though, from kicking the front gate again and again, breaking the lock open with sheer force. By the time he fled, he was exhausted and frail and blood covered. He had this to say, "I didn't even look back, Belkys. I just ran 'cause, tu sabes, I didn't think I'd get away. I ran into the traffic because one way or another, I was getting home. Either my home in Regla or my home up in el cielo."

* * *

With my news sources exhausted, I turned to the detective for more information on Madely's whereabouts. She wasn't exactly eager to share her notes, and I was afraid that if I pushed the matter, she'd become suspicious of me, so I took matters into my own hands. Two weeks after the footage of Madely's disappearance aired, I left MIA after a long, shitty day of angry customers and drove to Madely's home. It was late, and since nobody had lived in the house for some time, all the lights were off. To avoid suspicion, I parked down the street and walked, ducking under the fraying police tape. The front door was open. "Madely!" I called out, as if she'd actually be there. Of course, she wasn't, but I still felt her there with me. How could I not? It was her home, after all.

In This World of Ultraviolet Light

Of all the rooms in that house, I was most drawn to Palacio's—what had been, for much time, the unused nursery room. When I opened the door, the stench of the place hit me hard; it was ammonia, piss, unbearable. Still, I dealt with the stench and entered and marveled at Palacio's living conditions. The only comfort in the room was a twin-sized mattress in the center, stained and without linens. Coiled along the floor was the chain and the collar that Palacio had described on the news, likely resting where he'd last left them. The hole in the ceiling from where Palacio had tried to escape was somehow much smaller than I'd imagined it. It seemed impossible that anyone would fit through there. Plus, I hadn't even considered the insulation, a bright orange, bulbous material bleeding from the gape in the hole. And on the windowsill was Madely's strap-on beside a towel and oil.

I picked up the collar, put it around my neck, and tightened it. I did this because I wanted to feel what Palacio had felt. Truly, hearing Palacio gush on and on about his captor, I'd wondered: *What if that were me?* But I didn't expect the collar to lock or for the mechanism to be so sensitive. When it did lock, and after I tried to yank it off myself or to pull the chain off the bars, I realized that I'd truly made myself a prisoner of her, and I half expected her to walk in, draped in the flag, singing. Each time I tugged at the collar, it tightened. Now, I felt intense pressure on my neck. I could feel my pulse and the tightening of my skin around my eyes. I was being slowly strangled.

I settled on the dirty mattress and allowed my situation to come into focus, breathing in slowly, worried that with one dramatic movement, I'd lose my air passage altogether. The only thing I could think to do was text the detective. I almost did, but I was embarrassed. I didn't want her to see this side of me. So I powered off my phone and sat there, trying not to make the tightening worse. I sat there, as Palacio must have for so many nights, waiting for Madely.

* * *

Back before Madely ended things with me, I spent many days in her home. For a while, I thought I'd moved in, spending consecutive nights at a time. It was such a luminous time in our lives, getting to know one another. The loss of her child intrigued me—how an egg could become attached to the wall of the fallopian tube and develop like that. It was always strange for me, to hear Madely refer to herself as a mother. I didn't see it that way, but she did—a child born the day it was surgically extracted and discarded. There was such a sadness in her, one she hid well. You only needed to ask *Why are so many rooms locked off?* to realize that something wasn't quite right. Those rooms! Madely had forbidden me from entering them, and I betrayed her trust. I can own up to that. One morning, she was asleep and half-drunk beside me. I climbed out of bed in the ridiculous leather-studded getup she'd asked me to wear, and swiped her keys from the nightstand. In the first room, I expected to open that door and find a small crib, toys, maybe even some soothing wallpaper—storks carrying babies swaddled in cloth and that kind of thing. But there was nothing. Just an empty room, the very room that, eventually, would come to serve as Palacio's prison cell.

But what I found in the next room chilled me. It was like being in one of those horror films when a mother loses a child and opts to keep the room as a living memorial, only this wasn't for a child. It was for her parents. And what frightened me was that it had been ten years since her family had fled back to Cuba—or that's what I had understood—and still the beds were unmade, the cabinets open. On a dresser, there was a note written in Spanish: *We are sorry this didn't work out for you. We love you. Mami y Papi.* That room, it was also like a prison cell: bars on the windows (not uncommon in Miami), multiple locks on the door (this was curious to me). And another thing. The closets were filled with her family's clothing, the dressers too. Even her family's shoes remained, tossed at the side of the bed. It was as if they'd taken nothing back with them to Cuba. It was as if, at any moment, they'd all come ambling back into her home, asking, *What's for dinner?* It got weirder. When Madely found me in the room, still in the studded outfit I'd woken up in, she looked over my shoulder, at those dressers cracked open and yelled, "Desgraciado! You have no right!"

She took off her chancleta and threatened me, as if I were her child, not her lover. She was a bull, that woman, driving me out until I was in her backyard, fenced and warm under the sun, pleading, "Madely, por favor," through the sliding glass door, as all of Miami's traffic circulated and buzzed around me, as chickens in her yard clucked at my ankles. She left me out there till noon, at which point she emerged naked herself—a molten volcano of a body—a gun in her hand, and seeing her point that gun at me made me piss my pants right there. I knelt. I begged for her forgiveness. I told her that I'd never betray her again, and this must have resonated with her because she put the gun down, smiled, and let me in. She bathed me, warm, and asked me to lie on my stomach.

"I still have to punish you," she said. So I followed her instructions, and she took out a belt, and whipped my ass with, thank God, the leather end of the uniform belt.

Afterward, I promised her I wouldn't go into that room again. We didn't last much longer after that, and it was my fault. On Mother's Day, the whole day went by, and I didn't mention her pregnancy. Not once. She was the one who had to bring it up, the two of us wrapped in each other's arms in bed, Madely crying like a baby. When I told her that maybe we could try for one, she broke my nose and asked me to leave, so I did, by foot. I walked the whole damn way home, nose bleeding bad. It was a bad day. When I made it to Nana's, she hardly recognized me. I hardly recognized myself in the mirror, worn, tired looking.

That must have been about how I looked when the detective found me trapped at Madely's home, the collar around my neck. She'd put a tracking device on my car, so she knew where I was. She'd suspected that I'd try something like that. When she found me, she didn't judge me. She helped me get out of the collar and led me out of that room. And we didn't talk about it.

I can love her for that—not making me feel ashamed.

Shortly after my little stint, investigators returned and uncovered something truly horrible: two bodies buried in her backyard. Coño, Madely. The detective told me everything before the news channels caught wind of it, and all I could think was *Where is she? Madely?* Sometimes, late at night, when I'm leaning into the detective and we're binge-watching something on Netflix, I think of her. I imagine her in Cuba, seeking out Palacio, looking for a way to save him in spite of himself, and when I think of her this way, I remember what it was like to have that collar around my neck. Perfection. In some ways, I resent the detective for saving me, and I can't shake the feeling that the investigation is not over—like she knows I gave Madely the tip-off, and she's using me to get to her.

Every time I get that suspicion, I feel crazy.

But she knows about the text. She has to.

4

The Roasting Box

At the dead end of the Miami River—a levee divides the river's scrap metal industry from the passageway to Lake Okeechobee—wrecked cars are crushed and stacked along the banks. Iron oxide powder settles on nearby windshields and walls; when it rains, the rust and the oil on the streets bleed into the river. Pickup trucks with chain-link fences bolted to their beds line up at weigh stations. They're stacked with old refrigerators, corroded ironwork, obsolesced doorknobs—all the industrial junk that makes our living civilized. I've come here to sell my grandfather's junk.

Cigarette smoke and exhaust linger at the scrap metal lines, as does the static of distant radio stations. Cargo planes descend on the nearby airport, slicing over the river traffic. The scavengers weigh in twice, one at a time; first fully loaded, then again when they've dumped all their scrap. They're handed a PIN on a printed receipt. They sit around a makeshift ATM, waiting for an opportunity to cash out and repeat: $7, $42, $79. Compactors mangle some of the junk, but most of it is collected by large hydraulic cranes and placed on small container ships, which make their way down the river, past the high-rises in downtown Miami, toward the Caribbean islands.

Children fish on the north end of the levee. Ignoring the warning signs, they climb the fences, tossing their lines over the yellow floating oil booms, holding their rods and smelling all that pork in the air. Nearby, some families raise pigs. Outdoor terraces are converted into illegal slaughterhouses. Bones and carcasses are tossed in the river. Roasting boxes, Cajas Chinas, are stacked and sold along Okeechobee Road. During the holidays, festive lights and music illuminate the bloody terraces. Parents bring their children, who know that when choosing a holiday pig to bleed out, the larger ears are often the crispiest. On Noche Buena, pigs are nested in wooden roasting boxes to be cooked beneath a bed of charcoal. Neighborhood streets reek of pork. Family elders sit around la Caja China, engulfed in lechon smoke, drinking cheap beer, checking the pig's tenderness, the glow of the charcoal flickering against their wrinkled faces.

In the heat of my grandfather's shed lay things accumulated over the years: lawn mowers caked in grass sap, their motors burned out; birdcages rusted and stacked on their sides, still clinging to faded little red feathers; bags of charcoal ripped open by rats, lumps of coal and lighter fluid residue scattered across the floor. When he passed away, we couldn't get in. When we'd open the door, his things tumbled out. My grandmother sealed it shut with a string. It became a breeding ground for pests, and they brought snakes.

I cleared the shed, taking the snakes out with a machete chop to the head, as my grandfather had taught me. He'd trapped one, its body banded orange, yellow, and black, and he handed me his machete. Crouching, he pointed at white buckets. "Corta la," he said, "con fuerza!" When he dragged the buckets out of the way, the snake recoiled, struck at midair, then slowly slithered across the shed. I brought the machete down on the shed floor, manically, missing the snake with every strike. Would I find its bones?

Peeking through the cages, rising above the shovels, the wheelchair, the dried roses, was his Caja China roasting box, pressed up against the back wall. Its plywood blossomed from rot. The grease of holidays past had bred an infestation of palmetto bugs. The red Caja China logo had long since faded into wood. In all those years, he'd never taught me the art of roasting a pig.

To reach the box, I had to clear most of the shed. I rolled out the lawn mowers, dragged the birdcages onto the lawn. I poured buckets of standard nuts and bolts on his work area; they were filled with roaches, and as I sorted the consumables by their respective measurements, the brown, pearly eggs rolled off the work area and into the gaps in the floorboards. No sooner would I find the roaches hiding in some container or crevice—our old tackle box, even—than they would disperse and vanish through the floorboards or in the dark spaces within the shed. When I finally grabbed the roasting box, its wood crumbled in my hands. Only the aluminum frame and grease trap were intact.

Using an old wheelbarrow with a flat tire, I pushed the scrap through his yard, digging into the grass he'd cultivated when they'd just purchased the home. It used to be that the yard was all sand and gravel, but my grandfather had a way of making things grow. He brought the earth in the back of a pickup truck, planted tropical fruit trees from the seeds of fruits he'd eaten—mangos, bananas, avocados, coconuts, mameyes, fruta bombas. The trees grew and produced, and his yard transformed into a lizard-thick jungle with too much fruit for my grandparents to eat. They packed their refrigerators with fruit, gave each visitor a grocery bag filled with it. At the end of the season, two or three garbage containers of rotting fruit set at the curb for sanitation to take.

The receipt from Miami Scrap Metal was for $7. Somehow, I thought these things were more valuable. My grandmother refused the money when I offered it to her. She insisted that I keep it: "Los mayores cuidan los menores," she said.

Leaving the scrap metal site that day, sitting in traffic on the Thirty-Sixth Street bridge, I saw a young boy and an older man fishing in the river, as my grandfather and I had done years ago. They were oblivious to the traffic and the pollution, to all the things above and below them, slowly slithering about. They just fished, quietly, under the sun.

5

Stand Your Ground

After my shift, Rafa would scoop me up, and then we'd go vandalize people's homes. Every night, it seemed, we were rolling through the city of Miami, Petey Pablo blasting, a couple of spiked cherry Slurpees in our hands. We'd take turns leaning out the passenger window, swinging baseball bats at mailboxes, knocking them clean off. Or we'd dash onto strangers' lawns—in places with names like the Gables or Cocoplum—knocking over fountains and peeling out. We were addicted to breaking things. In a time when it seemed like anything could break, we were intent on making sure.

We liked toppling fountains the best; they were the stupidest ornaments. But this kind of vandalism had its risks. It took quite some strength to get under so much stone and water and lift. If you weren't careful, you could trip on all the wires and lights, or, worse, parts of the fountain could cascade on you, and then you'd have to get the rubble off before escaping. This happened to Rafa once—a big old five-tier toppled right on him. I had to get out of the car and help the mother-fucker, and lucky for us, the owners didn't hear the commotion. They didn't reach for their gun and meet us on the lawn, stand-your-ground style, or maybe I wouldn't be here telling this story.

This was Miami, in or around the months following the September 11 attacks. All of the city was covered in those two-dollar Home Depot American flags, and I don't why—but something about seeing those colors draped over the city made me and Rafa want to rip out every last one of them. Maybe that's how all this vandalizing started, with me and Rafa driving around collecting flags, collecting so many that in a week we filled four garbage bags' worth. And when we didn't have space for so much patriotism, we drove to the Everglades, set them atop cardboard, and burned them all and watched as the wind carried them, still burning, into the dry grass across Tamiami Trail.

* * *

We were students at Florida International University—first years. I was circling the drain around the business school; Rafa wasn't even attending some classes. We'd sat next to each other during orienta-tion, and, poor guy, some righteous-acting adviser took to the stage to patronize us all: *Wake up, kids! You're in college now. You've got to have a plan to succeed.* Dude was up there, shouting out these clichés, try-ing to rouse the masses, when, out of the blue, he pointed to Rafa and asked, "How about you?" Rafa, who was maybe the only darker guy in the crowd, was not having it. The man asked, "What's your major?" He even jumped off the stage to thrust the mic in Rafa's face.

And what did my childhood friend say, still yawning and rubbing his eyes from the boredom? "Guy, I don't know."

Well, that must have been the answer that the un-motivational speaker had been hoping for because the dude fixed his bowtie and said, "You don't know? Your major? What a way to start college."

He hit the mark, though. Neither of us were off to a good start. I was still clocking in thirty-plus hours at Walgreens—at the threshold of full-time work—trying to do my part to help my mom. I had no time to study. Plus, it was so hard to take college seriously. In one lab, we spent the first two weeks measuring the distance between the anus and the mouth of various mollusks. It seemed like one giant joke. In lectures, I could hardly stay focused, and I was certain that I would flunk out by the end of the year. And Rafa, he was doing just as bad. In some Latin American history course, he was learning about castes and colonialism and how sexual violence gave rise to economies of legitimacy, and rather than feeling empowered with that knowledge, he was coming unstitched.

In his creative writing course—when asked to describe something tangible in the room—he'd chosen his own hand, its color, a café con leche, and just thinking of the sugar drove his imagination to the Cuban countryside, the plantations, the hands of his ancestors ragged from the machete handle and the culling of sugar cane. Rafa had said that merely reading the poem aloud made his eyes watery, and he laughed about it, about being a dude on the brink of tears. But then his demeanor changed when he described the professor's feedback: *Nice. Imaginative. But the assignment was to focus on something tangible in the room.* "Was I not sitting right there," Rafa asked, "in front of him?"

"He probably meant something physical, you know?"

"What? So you agree with him?"

"Ay, Rafa," I told him. "You can't take things so personally."

"Oh yeah," he said, and he told me what happened next. Some dude shared a poem dedicated to a female student in the class. My first thought: *That's kind of cool.* I'd never thought of using poetry for anything like that, and I joked that maybe I should start writing poetry too. But Rafa was angry, and I didn't know why. Maybe I was distracted or bored, but he was getting all worked up over lines from this dude's poem: "firm as mangoes" and "bruised and sunburst" and "begging for a bite." I didn't mind the imagery, to be honest, and I told Rafa as much, and, at this, while walking through campus, right in front of everyone, he said, "Fuck you."

"What? Why?"

"Because you don't even know how ignorant you are," he said with such authority.

"I like mangos."

"The woman walked out of class. He was writing about her body, idiot."

Harsh! Something was changing in him. We'd be watching television or something—like we'd done a gazillion times—and J.Lo would come on in some performance, and I'd say, "Look at that ass," and Rafa would smack me really hard.

"Dude, do you gotta be like that?"

I guess he thought I was objectifying her. I'd only said it 'cause we'd always said shit like that when we saw J.Lo.

It didn't take long to feel like we were on the outs with one another. The school year had barely gotten rolling, and he'd started hanging out with new people: the kind of people who'd stand outside fraternities in the heat with signs like "Real Men Take No for an Answer" and "My Dress Does Not Mean Yes." I made fun of him for that, and he didn't appreciate the jokes. More so, from what I could tell, he'd stopped going to class entirely. Every night, I'd be like, *Yo, Rafa. We got to make some time to hit the books, you know. It's been a while.*

I missed him, if I'm being totally honest. I'd grown up with the guy my whole life. But he had no interest in studying, and the things he said scared me. One time he came right out and responded: "What for? What can college even really offer me?" Then after a long pause, he said, "You know what I miss? Driving around and fucking things up."

So that's what we did. Every night.

By the time the Twin Towers fell on September 11, neither me nor Rafa were particularly shook. If I'm being totally honest, it was such a huge fucking relief—that the world could end.

My parents were at work already. Rafa was over, and we were having leftover Taco Bell for breakfast, watching the buildings fall to A Tribe Called Quest's "Can I Kick It?" Even if my manager hadn't called to say the store was closed, I wouldn't have shown up. I wouldn't have shown up to class either. After breakfast, Rafa and I drove to the beach. We walked the shore and smoked, and he asked, "Can we do what we want now? Do we have permission?"

It seemed that way. It seemed like the tragedy had cleaved a hole in Miami large enough for us to hide in. It was the first time that I looked

In This World of Ultraviolet Light

at Miami, its skyline, and thought, *Would it be so bad if the planes had all crashed here?*

*   *   *

Down the street, there was this Muslim kid named Sohail—a tall high school senior who loved sneakers and *Star Trek* T-shirts. He was, by all accounts, a giant dork. Neither me nor Rafa had ever given him much attention, even if we were neighbors, but after the attacks, we started hanging out. He was good for scoring an ounce on short notice. So, one thing led to another, and before long, he was part of the crew. We'd even take him to vandalize things, and, boy, was he a menace to society.

One time, while sitting in a drive-through at McDonald's and waiting for our food, he jumped the fence into the playground and, under the cover of night, ripped a Ronald McDonald statue out from the ground. How he didn't get caught—how any of us didn't—I have no clue. Because next thing I knew, food in hand, we pulled up by the playground, and there was Sohail, popping the trunk and loading Ronald into the back of Rafa's Ford Bronco. It was such an excellent night, cruising around town, jamming with McDonald himself in the back. But when the party was over, we had to say goodbye. We drove up to the top of the Rickenbacker Causeway—a tall bridge that arches over Key Biscayne—and we threw it off and into the current, watched it bob and drift out into the dark.

That's how things were when Sohail would join us. He didn't just want to destroy mailboxes; he wanted to set them on fire. And he didn't care much for the small decorative fountains that people kept out in their yards; he was more interested in the large and extravagant public ones. In fact, it was Sohail who in November toppled the Coconut Grove Mall fountain at the peak of dinnertime and narrowly escaped as the community's heightened security descended on him. Just to be an asshole, he did it shirtless, wearing a black turban and yelling, "*Yayayayayaya!*" The guy even made the news: "Muslim Terrorist Targets Fountain in Coconut Grove." It was legendary, and we all had a good laugh. So, understandably, we were saddened when Sohail stopped hanging out with us. Dude wouldn't even pick up his phone. Turned out his parents had found his stash. By the time the holidays were upon us, he was so grounded, he couldn't even look out his window when we'd tap.

By then, most of Miami had unboxed their Christmas decorations. All of the city shimmered at night. It was merriment galore: so many lights, so many inflatables and Nativities and you name it. It was enough to make us forget about flunking out and dead-end jobs and all the injustices we'd witnessed in college. We suspected that's what the decorations were for—to hide all the ugly of the world and help us stay distracted. How badly the country wanted to move on. The sentiment was everywhere.

The media insisted that we not let the terrorists kill Christmas too. Politicians proclaimed: *Be brave. Go shopping. Your country needs you.* Even with the White House closed to the public, Laura Bush hauled in Christmas trees and continued the tradition with the theme "Home for the Holidays." There were stories of generous men, one who even traveled from Missouri to New York City with a wad of Benjamins, giving one to anybody who looked needy. And these stories worked. We forgot about the fear, the vulnerability. We were too merry to pay attention as security measures increased or to see George W. escalating tensions with Iraq. None of that mattered to us. The only thing we mourned was that Sohail was grounded, and we were without weed, and we didn't know what to do.

We were bored. Everywhere we looked, there were decorations too joyous and beautiful to smash, until one day there was only Christmas nonsense on the radio, and we were jamming to "Last Christmas" for like the fifth time, and I said, "Rafa. Bro, pull over." So he did, and I walked right through someone's winter wonderland of a yard, right up to a plastic Santa, the same rosy-nosed kind my parents had when I was a kid, and I punched it in the face—my knuckles crushing through into the hollow illuminated space. It was glorious. My fist was bleeding, and Rafa was laughing and hollering. And looking around at the strings of lights, the inflatable snowmen, and the rows of candy canes, I knew what we'd do next. We'd turn our attention from fountains to smashing Santas.

* * *

In This World of Ultraviolet Light

We started out small, yanking Christmas lights off trees and roof-tops. One night, we realized that we could redecorate people's homes so that it seemed all those decorations were having an orgy. It was an utter bacchanalia, what we were after. We could have an illuminated deer humping the Virgin Mary, and we could have Santa humping the deer, and we could duct tape Jesus and his little pecker to Santa's face. The possibilities were endless. And at around the time that some shit-face British dude hid an explosive in his shoe—on a flight to Miami—we really hit our fucking stride. It was classic.

Our favorite activity, dubbed "football practice," involved tackling the inflatables. It's super fun. Just find a neighborhood that's Christ-mas heavy, you know, and you park at one end. Then you walk over to the other end. This works best when it's you and a friend because you can race and you can keep a tally of how many figures you've tack-led. Rafa and I would line up, each on different sides of the street, then we'd count to three and begin the mayhem, diving into every inflatable character along the way, grabbing Santas and body-slamming them or jumping right into Mickeys' faces. Even if these are sacks of air, the activity could be a bit iffy. Because most of those inflatables are actu-ally anchored to the ground. When you tackle them, the anchors come loose, and they can gouge the living shit out of you. It happened to me—luckily, only nicked me, but got my jeans good. I dragged Mickey half a block. The fucker wouldn't let loose. When I jumped in the truck, I took him with me.

Like anything, though, eventually the thrill of Christmas bashing grew dim, and we began to eye larger targets. We spent a weekend vis-iting local dealerships at night and slashing their mega-giant inflata-bles—the kind you could see blocks away. Those were so dense with air that when we'd try and tackle them, we'd just bounce right off. That's why we used my steak knife. My favorite thing: when the big ones start to come down, it looks like they're going to crush you; they just buckle over and descend upon you from like twenty feet in the air, and there's no thrill like running wildly with all that hot air blowing up dust and dirt. Did it make me a little sad? Sure. I'd been a kid once. I knew what it meant to pass one of those mega inflatables on the highway, parents bickering, a little hope and Christmas cheer looming over the whole stretch of the city. But fuck it. In our headspace, we needed it. Hell. Given the chance, I'm not sure we'd have balked at hitting one of the towers.

Maybe we would have destroyed Christmas that season for all of Miami, but one night, on a routine job rearranging someone's yard, cops showed up. They rolled into the neighborhood real slow-like, lights off, and we didn't even see them until they were up close. It was Rafa, in fact, who shouted, "Pigs!" Lucky for us, we'd become cautious, and we'd parked on another block, so by the time the police lights blasted on, we'd already dipped over a few yards into our getaway, and we'd fled. But that next morning, we were heated. All the news channels took a break with the Muslim extremist bullshit to cover our Christmas bashing. It was a big news story. Reporters had descended on all of Miami, interviewing people, collecting surveillance tapes. The police even put out a reward for anyone with more information that could lead to an arrest. Suffice it to say, we were in deep shit.

And rather than venturing out each night to kill the town, we'd gather around the TV at Rafa's place and watch the news. Seeing kids sob and tell their stories about ruined Christmases made us a little sad, of course, but we also loved the attention; we loved the feeling of having done something in secret, of having gotten away. Sometimes the news stations would play grainy videos of us in action, and it was glorious; it was like reliving the Christmas bashing. And there was something else that was happening: our violence was bringing the community together. Neighbors were chipping in and replacing each other's broken Christmas decorations. "Look," I'd told Rafa, "it's like we're the spirit of Christmas." But the attention scared us plenty, so we stopped, kind of.

* * *

The last time we fought Christmas was at the start of the spring semester. Anyone with decorations still out, we'd reasoned, deserved a bit of ultra-vandalism. I'm not sure what got us back into smashing Santas. I remember that we were watching W.'s State of the Union Address, and he'd said something about an axis of evil, and Rafa had said, "You know what would be an axis of good?"

Since I'd known Rafa all my life, I knew just what the answer was: "Tell me Christmas bashing!"

I know what you're thinking. How could we outdo ourselves? What was there beyond football practice and the toppling of mega inflatables at the dealership? In truth, not much. But there was something unresolved. It was more of a joke, certainly not something that would draw attention. I still remember when the seed of this idea came to me. We were circling our own block, sharing a joint, and I said, "Isn't it strange that *his* house is the only one on our block not decorated?"

"Sohail?"

"Yeah," I said. "Everyone around here decorates like mad."

Rafa laughed. "Yeah, man. Fucking Christmas central, bro."

"Know what? We should decorate his place. Just imagine how he'd react."

"Bro," Rafa said, driving right past it, blunt in hand. "Yes! But you really want to eat where you shit? We never done nothing like this in our block. I don't know. I don't . . . What do you think?"

"I think he'd love it. I think it'd make his grounding more enjoyable," I said, but then I second-guessed myself. We were wanted, after all. And I told Rafa that we should definitely hold off, even if we missed the dude. Still, it didn't stop us from joking about it. It should have stayed a joke.

So when we did venture back onto the vandalism circuit on January 29, we were in good spirits. We thought of ourselves as custodians of the city, picking up the mess left over by Christmas. We plucked some of those lighted deer from the Biltmore Hotel—only the best for Sohail. Then we swung by the Church of the Little Flower, which has this super nice life-size Nativity. It was all a bit much to take, but we managed to pluck out the whitest little Baby Jesus, Mary, and Joseph. On the way back to our block, we stopped here and there, gathering strings of light and inflatables. Then, near Coral Park, we saw the coolest thing: a pink flamingo figurine with a Santa hat, all lit up. And it wasn't the cheap plastic variety. This was a woodcut, beautifully crafted, smooth to the touch. So we ripped that bad boy out, slid it over the rest of our booty, and, feeling good, went to Sohail's place.

It must have been three in the morning. This time of night, our block was dead. We parked under a tree, in the little shade blocking the moonlight, and feeling quite comfortable and at home, we set out to decorate Sohail's place the best we could. We envisioned a Christmas palace—the kind of house that all the people of Greater South Florida would pilgrimage to just to see. What a shame that Sohail's family didn't decorate. Their yard was perfect for it: lots of grass, just a few palms. We found the perfect place for the Nativity, in a bed of white and pink petunias surrounded by mulch.

Since we hadn't been able to fit the cow and sheep and the donkey in the truck, we situated the deer around the Nativity, and the pink flamingo too, as witnesses to the birth of Christ. All along the walkway, we anchored down inflatables of every variety, but we held off on plugging them in. Because we didn't want to draw attention to ourselves. We worked silently, wrapping lights around palm trees and attaching all these cords together with the extension cords we'd swiped. Before we plugged it all in, Rafa and I stood there, proud of the work we'd done. We bumped fists, and he said something like, "We've been breaking things so long, I forgot what making something felt like." He was right. I took the end of the electrical cord—the master cord that we had managed to attach everything to—and I walked it over to the side of the house where I knew there was an outdoor outlet.

I plugged it in, and, Jesus, it was gorgeous. The fans in the inflatables whirred, and the bags of air stirred and rose. That's when I noticed the pigs—fucking devils. They'd been smart this time; they'd likely parked further down the street to avoid detection. All that time, we'd been decorating, and little did we know that there were four officers closing in on us. Rafa was standing right in front of the doorway, really relishing all of it. It was the most joy I'd seen on his face in years. But I needed to warn him that we were busted, and I didn't know what to do. If I ran out toward him and yelled, it would reveal my position and I'd get busted too. If I fled, then I'd feel guilty for letting him take the blame. And as I breathed and tried to control my heart rate and thought through what course of action I should take, I heard the front door to Sohail's house open, and I saw the shadow of a man cross over Rafa. It was Sohail's father, and he was holding a gun—a fucking real-life gun.

In This World of Ultraviolet Light

Sohail's dad must have been scared, especially with all that anti-Muslim shit the media was spewing. And maybe building a Nativity on a Muslim man's house was a tad insensitive. Couldn't he see, though, how funny it was? Couldn't he see how much such a prank would make his son laugh?

I don't know how else to make sense of it. Because next thing I knew, the pigs drew their weapons. One stepped into the light and shouted, "Put that down. Right now!" Sohail's father, barefoot, shirtless, and only in his plaid boxer shorts, was trembling. He knew what I didn't know then. It took Trayvon Martin and Markeis McGlockton and Jordan Davis and all the other casualties for me to know why Sohail's father looked like he could piss his pants. So when he eventually did put his weapon down and motioned as if to say something, an officer tazed him unconscious.

And Rafa, who was already on his knees, hands behind his head, gave me a look as if to say: *Just run, man. No use in us both going down.* But where could I run to? I saw Sohail step into his yard, sporting his *Star Trek* pajamas; the guy was utterly dazed by the lights and the cops and the whole of it. He collapsed on his father and sobbed, and I saw another cop draw his weapon, so I hid behind the AC unit, and I waited all night. Because I was scared. I waited for the police and the ambulance to leave, and when all was clear—when Rafa had been taken into custody, his truck impounded—I walked home, showered, and then, drove to campus to measure mollusks and their fucking assholes.

6

The Phone Thieves

The bartender's Nokia 7260 is a cool fucking phone. Sleek—red trimming on the sides. Lightweight. Better battery life than my Ericsson. Her phone automatically accesses Yahoo when she holds down zero. It takes pics. Has a flash and everything.

She usually tucks it into the elastic on her shorts, but today she left the phone between two clean ashtrays. Now those ashtrays are overflowing, smoldering. She digs through the ash, rakes her fingers across the bar top. "My phone," she says. She digs some more, then slams her palm on the bar. "Fucking balseros," she says. "Did you see them? Did you see those refs?"

She isn't talking to me. She's pacing back and forth, rubbing her face, drawing trails of ash down her cheeks. Now she's washing her hands in ice, the strap of her tank sliding off her shoulder. "Fuck my life," she says.

A calypso player beats his pan; he sings toward the bay. The bartender hates that guy. Usually she throws lemon wedges at him, laughs about it, how utterly oblivious that guy is, beating his pans. But today she says, "Fuck the calypso player," and she chugs her pilsner.

"Which balseros?" I ask. "Which ones took your phone?"

But she doesn't hear me. She dries her hands on a towel and then digs through the ashtrays again, raking her fingers across the bar top like she might have missed it.

The calypso player beats his pans, oblivious. I feel oblivious too, because I didn't notice the thieves. I might have noticed if I didn't have to pee all the time. Enlarged prostate. A few beers and there's no holding back. It's a slow burn, the way it just drips out. They probably took her phone during one of the many instances when I dripped into the urinal, painfully.

Now I lean over the bar, call her over. "Describe the balseros," I say.

The bartender looks at me like she's never seen me before, like she hasn't been serving me three Stellas, three times a week, forever. She sits on her stool, lights a cigarette, and then looks past me to the bay, as if she could see them out there, fleeing to Cuba with her phone.

Weather's shitty. It's been this way for weeks—not good for an outdoor bar in Bayside. She's blowing smoke into the bay, the rain, the mist. Miami's skyline is hardly visible through it all, but she's gorgeous—the pilsner goes straight to her hair, her eyes, her skin. I want her.

She hasn't said it, but I know she's been under the sun lately: her burnt shoulders, the pale lines running down into her tank. I thought I saw her at the beach last week, walking along the shore in an army-green two-piece. I thought I saw her at the grocery story, pushing around a cart filled with two-liter bottles of Coke and flopping around in yellow Crocs. I thought I saw her in traffic, waving at me through the tinted glass of a Ford Focus. "Hey, I thought I saw you . . ."

"It's gone," she says. "Fuck my life."

"Try calling it."

"Try calling it?"

"Try."

"How stupid can they be?"

"I'll call it then," I say, pulling out my phone. "Give me your digits."

"Digits? Who are you, man?"

"I'm just trying to be nice."

"Sure you are," she says and walks away. But after a little while she returns, leans closer to me, and says, "Sorry. Customers hit on me all the time. You want me to call, then I'll do the dialing." She stands, leans over the bar, takes my phone, and dials. No answer.

"Try again," I say. "Try a few times."

No answer. No answer. "No answer," she says and slides my phone back.

"At least we tried," I say.

"You better delete my number."

"I will."

"You better."

"I will."

"Fucking balseros."

"I know," I say. "Fuck them."

The bartender unplugs her charger and tosses it in the trash. It's really raining now, curtains of it coming across Bayside. Patrons close out their tabs, run off into the storm. The calypso guy doesn't pack up his equipment, but rather continues banging his pan. "Fuck the calypso player," she says and laughs. Thunder booms far off. When it's just me and her sitting under the aluminum canopy listening to the rain fall and the music, I order another beer. She pops it open, slides it over. Then she digs through the ashtray, rakes her fingers through it.

"I'm in insurance, you know?" I say. "Was the phone insured?"

She paces back and forth. Sits on her stool and lights another cigarette.

"Was it insured?" I ask.

But she's ignoring me again, looking out at the bay.

"Fucking balseros," she says.

Later, driving home, I dial her number again. I know! I should have deleted it, but what does it matter? It rings. No answer. Just her voicemail greeting: *It's me. Leave a message.*

* * *

It's still raining when I get to my apartment—a small, carpeted space in downtown. Now that I have a real job, I can afford to live on my own. I'd left the windows cracked open for fresh air. When I enter, the vertical blinds are waving, rising, falling, crashing into one another. The claims I've been investigating have lifted off my coffee table and are whirling about the room. Maybe it's the beers, but I like this—the chaos, the smell of rain, the sight of all my busy work in disarray—and so I fall onto my couch, kick off my shoes, and close my eyes. I'm buzzed.

And I can't sleep. Occasionally I reach onto the coffee table, take my phone, and redial her number. It rings. No answer. Just her voice: *It's me. Leave a message.*

It's me. Leave a message.

It's me. Leave a message.

The blinds rise and fall. I'm in and out of sleep, listening to her voice. In the dark, the glow of the display screen mesmerizes me. And something about the wind and the blinds reminds me of the ocean's surf. I see her there on the beach, army-green two-piece tossed at her side. She's lying in the sand, golden, waxed, lathered in coconut tanning lotion. Her eyes are closed, her nipples shriveled and adorned with emerald rods. She's surrounded by seashells and coiled wires and the husks of cell phones, weathered shards—ruby, navy, hot pink. Balseros in frayed clothing run along the surf, scavenging, taking as much wire as they can as lightning drips down the horizon. In this dream, she opens her eyes—two bright displays—and says. "It's me. Leave a message. Leave a message. Hey! It's me. You better go to the bathroom. Go pee."

* * *

I wake to my phone vibrating. It's her number. I answer: "Hello."

"Deja de llamarme, maricón."

I don't say anything.

"Oye. Maricón. Me oyes? Hear me?"

"Who is this?" I ask.

"Qué coño, compadre? Deja de llamarme."

"Ladrón. Thief," I say. "You are the thief."

He yells, "Me cago en el coño de tu madre!"

"Ladrón," I yell.

"Ladrón? Estás confundido, comemierda. Esto no es tuyo."

"Do you realize that my girlfriend has been crying all day about this?" I say.

"Qué? Your girlfriend?" The voice laughs. "Esa gringa de mierda."

"My girlfriend. Mi novia."

"Tu novia, eh?"

And that's how it is, speaking to these people. Eventually, I ask him why he's stolen my girlfriend's phone. It feels nice to say it aloud. And would you know, the dude takes offence to my accusation. He claims that someone sold him the phone for forty bucks. I don't believe him, and when I press him further, he agrees to return the phone so long as I pay him for the trouble. Says he's tired of my calls anyway, that I should be screwing my girlfriend, not calling him. And even though the guy's full of shit—I even hear his accomplices laughing in the background—I agree to his terms, acting thankful and sincere, and I mark the address that he provides me with.

"No policía," he says.

"No policía," I confirm and hang up.

* * *

I'm surprised when I leave my building's parking garage that it's still dark—five in the morning. It's no longer raining, but the streets are flooded, and the palm leaves are swaying in the gusts.

From the high-rises in downtown, I drive toward the Miami River, to a neighborhood surrounded by junkyards. Most of the houses in this neighborhood are on the river, which is more detrimental to their value than most people would think—insurance companies won't cover these kinds of homes. The river itself is a channel for scrap ships and petroleum rigs. This close to the water, the houses deteriorate faster, especially since the river is mostly salt water now. Wood rots. Insects eat at the roof, the frames. Sometimes with heavy rains, the dirt on the riverbanks erodes, revealing bits of buried scrap: car parts, barrels, tires. This is a very poor neighborhood, where people use buckets for mailboxes. They spray-paint house numbers on exposed cinderblock. It's the kind of neighborhood I don't usually have a reason to visit.

Driving though these flooded streets, AC blasting, stirs up the familiar feeling in my bladder. Every dark corner, tree, post, bucket, seems an invitation. But I'm on a mission. I hold it.

Then, coming up on the address, I see a porch light. There are some men standing outside with flashlights. They shine their lights at me when I approach, so I pull over across the street.

Three young men stand shirtless at the entrance. One of them—shaved head, skin blotchy, black patches meshing into pink—rests his hands on an aluminum baseball bat. This kid's biting his lip, and he looks angry, worked up. The other two, twins, it seems, have their arms crossed; they're identical in every way—height, hairstyle, stance—except one of them has an eagle tattooed on his chest. Standing the way they're standing, the twins' nipples line up. All of these guys are grilling me, shining their flashlights at me, looking at me like they might punch in my face before handing over that phone. The kid with the bat taps the sidewalk with the aluminum end—that metallic sound slices through the neighborhood and into my bladder.

At this point, it's not that I want to be a hero anymore. I've really got to pee, so I get out of the car and walk right up to them, even if the sight of them scares me plenty.

"El dinero?" one of them asks as I approach.

"You mind turning those off?" I say. "Por favor."

"El dinero?" he says, tapping the sidewalk with his bat.

"Let me see the phone first," I say, stepping closer to them. One of the guys tosses me the phone. I fumble; it slides down the sidewalk into a puddle, but it doesn't break. "Shit," I say. Now I'm on my knee drying the phone off on my shirt. The phone's not broken though. I check the display: thirty-two missed calls. "I've got to pee so bad," I say.

"El dinero," they say.

I hand them the cash.

"This forty," one of them says. "We say ochenta por el teléfono."

"That wasn't our agreement."

"Ochenta."

I pocket the phone, sleek, step back from them and the light.

The kid with the bat steps closer. He's tapping the pavement, but he might as well be butting my bladder. "You give it," he says. "You leave it with you."

"What?" I search through my pockets, finds some loose bills, coins, totaling to about fifty-six dollars. "This is all I got," I say, handing them the cash.

The kid with the bat takes it, raises the bat, then enters the house.

"Dale las gracias," one of them calls into the house.

"A ese gringo de mierda?"

"You must excuse all of our friend," the guy with the tattoo says. "He speak English very poorly. What we are trying to say is thank you. Have a good night, okay."

The men shut off their flashlights and enter the house. I enter after them. It takes them a moment to realize that I've followed them into the house. The guy with the bat pushes me toward the door. "Bye-bye," he says.

"Bathroom," I say. "El baño."

"Bye-bye."

"Por favor," I say.

"You gonna shit?" he says and laughs. Then he makes a farting noise.

"Just pee."

"Qué dijo, acere?" one of the twins says.

"Tengo que usar el baño," I say. "I have to pee."

"Y porque no lo dijiste?"

"El baño, por favor?"

The guy with the tattoo eyes me, but nods and directs me to their bathroom. I rush through the living room, past a small domino table, and into the bathroom and slam the door.

The bathroom's disgusting—green walls, paint chipping, mold. Next to the toilet, someone's stapled pages from a dirty magazine: girls in heels, bent over, a giant target zoning in on their asses; breasts and more breasts, stacked one next to another by the faucet; women's faces, their eyes struck out with permanent marker, cocks drawn up alongside their lips. It makes me want to look through the bartender's phone. I flush; the toilet gurgles, nearly overflows. I wash my hands in yellowish water, dry them on my jeans for fear of the stiff rag on the towel rack. Somebody bangs on the door, yells, "Oye. No te pajas," and laughs. They all laugh.

*　*　*

When I exit the bathroom, the guys are sitting at the domino table drinking beers and watching a black-and-white movie on a small television. The furniture in the room is sparse, and it's clear from the stacks of worn clothing and blankets that at least one person sleeps on the burgundy couch by the front door.

"Cerveza?" the guy with the bat asks. He's snapped open a Natural Ice and set it at the table, even though I haven't asked.

I settle in at the table, push some fichas out of the way.

"Thank you, guys," I say. "I had to pee so bad."

They nod, drink from their beers.

I push the beer away.

I'm drawn to the fichas. They look authentic, made of animal bone. Inscribed on their backside is the Cuban flag. These are new Cubans. Twenty-first-century marielitos. Balseros, as the bartender had referred to them. I know because my mom tells me that these are the kinds of Cubans I need to stay away from. They live off the government, rob, cheat, leech off their relatives. Some of them drive out into the farmlands to butcher horses. They have no respect.

I sip from the beer to appease them, though it's late and I'm not particularly in the mood to drink anymore. What I want to do is get back to my apartment and look through the phone.

"Quieres jugar? Play?" one of them asks.

"Con un gringo?" the guy with the bat says.

"Los gringos son malísimo."

"Los gringos son los mejores," I say. "The best." I'm not sure why I've said it. I'm not really gringo. I'm Cuban, but not like them. And I love dominoes.

They laugh. Then I say, "You haven't played real Cuban dominoes until you've played with a Cuban gringo."

"A Cuban gringo? Quieres jugar, gringo?" they ask.

"No. I really need to go," I say.

"We play," the one with the bat says, finally setting it down against the wall and sitting across from me. "Amado," he says, offering his open hand. We shake.

One of them draws out some domino racks from beneath the table, says, "Aquí se habla Español." Then they rack up and play even though the sun is rising. They're not used to the way I play. And it takes Amado a moment to adjust to my style. Rather than systematically playing my strongest hand, I often start out by baiting the opponent's strong hand so that they deplete it. At first, nobody is quite sure what I'm doing. They jeer at me and Amado, but then we win. And we keep on winning. Something strange happens. We're playing dominoes, slamming fichas, teasing each other about our plays, and I'm not seeing the filth anymore. We are a machine, placing one ficha at a time, watching how it all turns out, each and every game, and it's a blast.

When it's almost eight, Amado gets up and starts getting dressed for work.

"What are you doing?" I ask. "We're winning."

"Trabajo," he says. Then he buttons on a McDonald's uniform, visor and everything. And he plays one more hand before he has to leave for work. We lose this time.

Now I'm leaving too. We all promise we'll play again, and we hug each other. I offer Amado a ride, but he insists on walking. When I drive away, they stand at the door of that dilapidated house, all shirtless except for Amado. A barge loaded with scrap passes behind them. It's been a long time since I've been around good people. But now it's just me and the bartender's phone. I touch it, and it lights up: thirty-two missed calls.

* * *

In my apartment, I roast a pot of coffee and sit at my counter looking down at the bartender's phone. This is the closest I've been to her. I've made a mental promise not to look through her phone, but it's hard to drink my coffee without prodding. I trace my finger along the silver S on the phone's face, pass my fingers over the keypad, and I activate the

In This World of Ultraviolet Light

display screen. Then I'm inside her phone, opening folders, and while I do this, something carnal overtakes me.

There are three photos saved on the device: there's one of her and her boyfriend; a view of Miami's skyline from the bay; and a picture of a fresh scar that runs from her belly button to her hip. I zoom in on her hip, her skin. I can see the whirl of her little hairs around the scar. As I'm moving about her stomach, the pic's interrupted by an incoming call—it's William White. I set the phone down, let the call go to voicemail, but it's vibrating all over the counter like it might get up and spin off. In that instance, I feel seen. I feel exposed, and I panic.

Once I'm sure there's no risk of answering the phone, I pick it up again and look through her contacts. There are eight: Marco Acosta, Daddy, Erica Losa, Alejandro Pla, Ximena Suarez, Tia Wilma, Robbie Rico, and William White. Of these, there's an extensive text message thread with Mario Acosta. Lots of lovey-dovey stuff, but there's also the occasional *Where are you? Fuck you. I needed you today.* Then there's the name, *Carina. Carina, you at the bar? Thank you, Cari. Cari the little Poopsie. I love you, Carina. I'm sorry, Cari.* And there's the calendar—all those visits to the doctor, all those bills to pay: Verizon, AMEX, Netflix, Ford, Sallie Mae. Her birthday weekend: March 15 through the 17th, marked by little green turtles. It's adorable.

Another call interrupts my browsing. This time it's Tia Wilma. I set the phone down, and I take my coffee and sit by the window. Though I live in a small apartment, I lean in just enough so I can see Biscayne Bay between the slit of two commercial buildings. Soon, this phone will be back at that little bar, between the apartment buildings; it'll be back in her soft hands again.

I'm not sure how Carina will react, but I like to think she'll be happy. She'll pull a barstool next to me and take my arm. She'll thank me for being so brave and kiss my cheek. There will be plans to hang out at my place. Fuck her boyfriend. Afterward, we'll lie in bed, going through our phones, our emails, occasionally glancing at each other and ducking beneath the sheets for more. We'll pick our own ringtones for each other: "Love Me Two Times" or maybe "Bold as Love."

* * *

In the evening, I put on my best dress shirt, tuck it into my jeans. I can feel the bulges, first of my phone in one pant pocket, but also Carina's in the other. I drive to Bayside, arriving in the lot at the same time as the calypso player.

The musician is trying to pull his gear out of his van. I approach the man to help, but he drops it, raises his fists, and threatens to punch.

"You think I'm a thief?" I ask.

"This is my equipment."

"No, dude. I was just offering . . ."

"Fuck off," he says, and he eyes me as I walk away.

Carina's at the bar, sitting on her stool. Weather's nicer today—blue metallic waters, gold and red infused in the clouds. There's a breeze coming in from the Atlantic, which makes the small posters and receipts Carina's stapled to the bar wall flutter.

It's still early, and most of the tourists at Bayside have yet to visit the bar. They opt for the stores, the restaurants, the one-hour boat tours on the bay. Party boats illuminated by disco lights cross the bar in the distance.

I sit, smile. "How are you?" I ask.

Carina smiles and stares into me, but just as quickly, she stares off like she's never seen me before. "What'll it be?"

When I don't answer, she sits on her stool, smoking a cigarette and poking at a small orange box. I take out her phone, lay it on the bar top, but she doesn't notice. She's ripping the cardboard off the box, then the plastic. She takes out a new phone; this one's a BlackBerry. She unravels the power cord, puts it to charge behind the cash register.

"You decided yet?" she yells across the bar.

The calypso player sets up by the water.

"Fucking calypso player," she says. "Same songs. Each night. Same shit. So you gonna have something or what?"

"Your name's Carina, right?"

She slides off the bar, steps up on something so she's looking down at me. "Who's asking?"

"I heard."

"Heard from who?"

"I just heard it."

In This World of Ultraviolet Light

"You following me around?" she asks, pointing at my face.

"What?"

"You heard me," she says. "You the one following me around?"

"I don't know what you're talking about. Why would I follow you around?" I ask.

"I know you," she says. "You're the guy that was asking me a zillion questions about my phone. Did you take it? Were you the one?"

"I'll take a Carina, please. Corona."

"You the one? You the fucking guy?"

"I didn't come here to be interrogated," I say.

"Creeps like you. Then get the fuck out of here," she says, tossing a lemon wedge at me and returning to her stool. "Get the fuck out of here. You don't know me. You don't know anything about me."

I push my stool back from the bar, stand.

"Go," she says. "Get out of here."

"But . . ."

"Go."

Before leaving, I take the phone from between the two ashtrays and pocket it. Now I'm walking along the bay, listening to calypso, feeling the shape of her phone against my thigh. She's throwing lemon wedges at me, casting me off like I'm one of the balseros.

In the car, I scroll through her phone. I know I can take it back to my apartment and look for more of her. I know I can do this all night until it dies in my hands.

7

Immaculate Mulch

Marjory walked along the creek with her 12-gauge, shooing the crocs back into their protected stretch of marsh and free living. It was a chilly morning, mist rising from the strand so that the palmettos on the adjacent bank looked like one monolithic organism. All was silent. Even the gators retreated into the water without a splash. Such landscapes, Marjory believed, were as useful as mosquitoes. Good only for making films. Throw in some Calusa Indians, a canoe, flutes and drums, and that'd be worth watching. But in life, she questioned the purpose of preserving such a place. The very notion of federal restoration confounded her. Could we really restore a slough? To what?

She stood at the very edge of the facility, site manager to the largest mulch-manufacturing site in the southeastern United States. Staring off into the blur of wilderness, she could feel the heat radiating off the acres of wood chip mounds behind her. The necks of the wood chippers towered over those piles, dormant. From up above, Christ would look down upon her site and see an artist's palette: reds, browns, blacks, and tans. Street-side, there were piles of lumber and slash and, honestly, whatever it was people had put on the curb for pickup the previous night. Even this early, the lot smelled of pine and manure and oil, and, if Marjory was being totally honest, she loved it. Because it all pointed to civilization—machine tracks on the caked mud, a line of roll-off containers freshly painted red, some dirty work gloves in the grass, a few porta-potties. If it were up to her, all the trees in the whole of the Everglades would be fed into those wood chippers—stray rodents and all—and sprinkled across every goddamned garden bed in this land of amber waves of grain.

And it being the first Friday of the month—a local client appreciation day and cookout—she'd arrived extra early to commandeer the picnic tables with her Party City tablecloths and that long sad banner, strung from one branch to another, which read: "We Appreciate You Very Mulch." If she'd failed to get there early enough, the bus would arrive and then the migrants would crowd the tables, leaving bags and empty soda bottles and all the rest of their mess all over the place. And if the workers left their messes, then the vultures would show up, followed by the usual alligators. Nothing but logs with teeth and shitholes, she liked to say. Opportunistic fuckers, no better than her workers—those Spanish-chirping little men from Mexico or Puerto Rico or who even knows.

She wheeled over the charcoal grill and set it up real nice by the tables alongside a couple of old coolers filled with beer. With her big floppy sun hat and her stubbly chin and long braided gray hair, she looked like one of those frontier women preparing to defend the homestead. And when the bus did arrive and the men disembarked, Marjory stood guard. "Buenos días, señora," they said, one face after another. They sounded like birds: *Señora, señora, señora. Buenos días, señora.* Couldn't they hear it? The way their words fell into the dirt and died there. Rogelio and Román, just two of her many wheel loader operators, walked past her on their way to start their shift, their helmets in their hands.

Román nudged his pal in the ribs and, smiling, shouted out, "¿Qué hay de comer?" They laughed, and though Marjory didn't know the meaning of his words, she could see their dumb joke coming a mile away.

She wagged her finger and shouted, "Nah. Not today, Hay-soos. Clients only."

Rogelio, who'd always stayed out of the jokes, shouted, "Una pantera! Señora! Una pantera! Corre!"

And Marjory, who was confused by the urgency in his voice and the growing commotion, by the way her workers proceeded to gather around like vultures, waiting for something to die, yelled back, "For fuck's sake. What's gotten into you all?" Sensing something was amiss, she even doubled-down and looked for any stray gators, thinking one of those sneaky fuckers had crawled up beside her and was fixing to chomp on a bit of her. But there was nothing. No threat. So she yelled that everyone should get back to work. And it was then, as she was really leaning into her authority as site manager, even staring some of those Mexicans down, that the Florida panther landed on her.

It'd been resting on a branch all morning, watching her work. In scaring away pests, she'd never thought to search the trees. But that's where the panther had been hiding, sand colored, invisible against the bark. It was a large cat, at least five feet long. They were rumored to be extinct or in such small numbers that nobody ever saw them. Even those that were chipped could hide so well that park rangers, knowing their exact location, would sometimes fail to locate them.

She thought the panther was a branch that had fallen until she smelled the musk and felt the warmth of its body against her own. When it stood on its fours and freed her from its weight, she tried to scoot to safety, and it was then that the panther lunged into her. It was trying to bite her neck and put an end to her flailing, but Marjory, through instinct alone, blocked with her arms. She kept smacking the animal in the jaw, trying to create even more space between her and the cat, but to no success. The panther was intent on eating her, and it was clear that there was little she could do to protect herself from it. When it bit her forearm, she yelled and cried and prayed to the Lord, and the

In This World of Ultraviolet Light

panther tugged so hard at this mound of a woman in the direction of the dirty creek.

It paused now and then, releasing her arm to bare its teeth at the spectators. In these moments, Marjory would try to crawl away, but it was no use. All the panther had to do was push its paw down on her and press its claws into her skin and she'd stop. She was certain that she'd die.

If it wasn't for Rogelio, who strapped on his helmet, then seized her shotgun, she'd be dead. It was a miracle, in fact, that she hadn't died already—that the panther hadn't crushed her windpipe. It was a miracle that it hadn't drowned her. By the time Rogelio shot, she'd been dragged into the creek. Alligators had taken interest, sneaking up toward her along the bank, waiting their turn.

Rogelio took the gun, aimed, and fired. He blasted a hole in the panther's face. Then the cat collapsed right there, right on her, and though Rogelio denies it—he claims to have pulled Marjory out from the water first—everyone saw what he did next. He dragged the panther out over the caked dirt and to the mulch. "Coño," he said, running his hand along its short hairs. "Que bonito."

Afterward, Marjory helped herself out from the swamp. She stumbled over to one of the picnic tables, her arm bleeding profusely, her face all clawed up. She didn't know what was worse, the pain radiating up her arm and on her face or the fact that those good-for-nothing men had all chosen to watch her die—except Rogelio. "Do I have to say it?" she shouted. "Get the fuck to work." As the men dispersed, she sat on the bench to try to calm her nerves.

Rogelio brought her the shotgun; he fetched her water from the cooler. "Señora," he said, "te mordió. Es malísimo. Tenemos que llamar a la ambulancia ahora mismo." Such an ugly language. It might as well have been a bunch of mosquitoes buzzing in her ears. The only word she understood, somewhat, was "ambulancia." Sometimes, she thought, all of the Spanish language could be spoken by adding an "ia" to the end of an English word, and it was something she did when she was barking orders, with phrases like *work faster-ia, check the inventor-ia,* and *the breaks over-ia.*

"I'm fine-ia," she said, and she poured the water over the several puncture marks on her arm. The sting of the ice dulled some of the pain. How she wanted to just go about her day. But her wounds were really bleeding out, and it was clear to Marjory, then, that she'd need to go get stitched up. Using a pair of scissors, she cut off a piece of her apron and, with Rogelio's help, wrapped her arm good and tight; she secured the bandage with a whole roll of masking tape, just looping it around her arm again and again to form a cast. The little pride she got from her handiwork put her in good spirits, and she said, "Ro-jelly-o. I'm sorry. You're right. I should see a doctor. But first . . ."

She went, holding the shotgun with one hand, to see the creature. It was a large beast, muscular looking. Christ! How it resembled those disgusting little short-haired cats people kept as pets. The thought of the panther using her mulch site as a litter box made her want to puke. She kicked the beast, and to her surprise, it extended its paw; the animal was alive, still breathing. She could see its fangs exposed in the place where its face had been obliterated, its long pink tongue. "Fuck you," she said, and she attempted to raise her shotgun, but with the pain, she could not.

"Ro-jelly-o," she said. "Come here. Shoot the fucker again."

"Pero, señora," he said, "es ilegal . . . te multaran hasta cien mil dólares."

"You already shot it once!"

"Pero, señora . . ."

Marjory knew he was speaking the truth. In addition to the fine, anyone who killed a Florida panther could also face up to a year in prison. Most of the folks in this part of the Estero community knew as much. Those feline pests of the Glades—inbred with mountain cats from the north—were more protected than the state's own citizenry. Hell, in the state's eyes, those cats were more human than her workers. She must have realized it then that in shooting the panther and saving her life, Rogelio had put something in motion much larger than himself. And even if he was a fucking Mexican, she didn't think he deserved to be fined or deported or imprisoned—not him. You take any of those other workers and who cares, but Rogelio had saved her life. She owed him.

In This World of Ultraviolet Light

If memory served her right, she'd always appreciated the man. It was Rogelio who one day during a torrential downpour offered her his umbrella. God! He was taller then. Or maybe that wasn't him at all. No, Marjory thought. He was the one who'd bring her mangos, leave them on her desk in the trailer—a real kiss ass. Or maybe he was the one she'd run into that one time while Christmas shopping, and he'd introduced her to his whole family as "la jefa." Oh, it was becoming clear that she didn't know Rogelio from Romero or Raul or Ricardo, and it didn't matter. That little Mexican man, with the faded Marlins shirt, and the one eye that was inconveniently staring off some other place—she would make sure he'd be taken care of for his deeds.

So she took a deep breath and she thought: *What would Jesus do?* And Jesus, of course, would call the Department of Fish and Wildlife and just take the blame for it all. For fuck's sake, they'd understand. In the meantime, she couldn't keep a dying panther around for the party—not on client appreciation day. So she told Rogelio to throw the panther in an empty roll-off; that's what he did.

While Marjory rushed off to the Estero Medical Center, blood seeping through her bandage, Rogelio used the wheel loader to scoop the panther and drop it into the red steel roll-off container. He waited for the clang, then, without even peaking in to check on the animal, he returned to work.

* * *

Marjory had phoned ahead so that her intern, Devon, could get started preparing the grillables. He just about flipped his shit when she alluded to the panther attack. He kept mumbling, "I don't get paid enough . . . at all." Doctors made her hang up in the midst of her instructions because of the "medical emergency," so the fate of the cookout was unclear. But before she hung up, she'd managed to tell Devon that if he led a successful cookout, he'd get an A, no questions asked.

Fucking doctors. They took hours to tend to her wounds. Probably 'cause none of them had ever seen a panther bite before. Even after they stitched her up good, she had to spend a good hour of her day in nothing but that hospital gown, ass flat on the chair, for observation. Doctors wouldn't release her otherwise—that word *release* made her mad, like she was the animal: "Say you'll release me one more time." And the whole hour, high on meds and watching the dewdrops on the window evaporate, she suspected that those docs were letting the ticker run so they could bill more hours.

It wasn't until about 1:00 p.m. that Marjory rolled back onto the mulch facility all stitched up and loaded on antibiotics and pain relievers. She was tickled to see the parking lot full—signs of a good turnout. Why the fuck not? It was a beautiful day; the cold had given way to the midseventies, and, boy, after the ordeal she'd been through, could she use a Bud Light and a plateful of sausages.

She recognized Tim Agee's truck right away 'cause of the nutsack dangling under the hitch. Agee was the largest potato farmer in Southwest Florida. The man owned acres and acres right up alongside the Fakahatchee Strand—hogged most of the migrant workers during the picking season. She'd been on his land before. Not a tree in sight. During the summer months, he was known to order enough mulch to protect all his spuds from the Florida sun, so you know he got a good deal.

She also recognized Charles Black's big red truck. He was the facilities manager to Ave Maria University, a real motherfucker. Last time she'd seen him was at the shooting club; him and his pals were drinking tequila and skeet shooting, and Henry, the president of the club, had to walk over there and suspend their membership. The wokies already had their feelers fixed on recreational gun use, and there was just no place on a shooting range for liquor anymore. How he got that prestigious job at the university—at a Catholic university—she had no clue. Probably screwed someone in HR. If there was anything Charlie was good for, it was his big dick and thighs 'cause the rest of him was as dumb as Janet Reno. And, of course, how could Marjory forget? The sinner was also good for five thousand to nine thousand yards' worth of premium mulch every summer, depending on the hurricane season.

From the trucks alone, she knew that Hank Palmer was there, the buyer at Legar Builders. Jeremy Graff was probably there, the facilities manager to Collier County Public Schools. And who else? Of course! The teal-blue Jeep Wrangler. Mike Miller! He owned small gardening stores in every county except Miami-Dade, which was too bad 'cause that's where he started the business. After Castro came into power, he just packed up his American flag and drove west and started over.

These days, it seemed like respectful folk were packing up all over the place and trying to find their own. Most had taken to Twitter. Marjory couldn't stand social media. The abyss of different opinions terrified her, how at any moment some liberal wokie could manifest out of the blue, demanding attention and pronouns and you name it. What did the memes even mean? She preferred the cookout, the greasy burgers, the melted cheese, the ketchup, the Styrofoam plates. This was *her* space, her time to talk immigration and gun rights and the lack of respect shown to the police, and she could do this while drinking beer and not once feeling the urge to look over her shoulder. Being around these men in such a candid setting—these wealthy movers and shakers of Estero—made Marjory feel, truly, a sense of belonging, something that hadn't been easy to come by.

When she first moved to Estero with her husband of four years, she was a different woman. While he was off at the power company, she was expected to tend to the house. Out of boredom, she joined a women's group at a Christian church. Her and the other wives would gather on Tuesday afternoons for coffee and doughnuts to discuss issues in the community. Some of them brought their babies, all cute looking and frilly. This was a different era, long before the migrant booms. Coming from Arkansas, she took to the humidity nicely, and she really enjoyed how quaint and precious it was to drink coffee in little mugs in a sunlit room, talking about Jesus. She seemed to be getting along just fine until one day, the group brought forth a topic from the priest himself. The ladies were to discuss whether the church should sponsor ten Cubans who had migrated illegally to Miami via the Mariel boatlift. For Marjory, this was a clear and shut case: absolutely not!

But the ladies disagreed. "Whoever is kind to the poor," one of them said, "lends to the Lord."

And as they nodded in unison, Marjory set her mug down on the wood floor and asked, "Lends what?"

The ladies seemed confused. Another volunteered the answer: "Marjory, we'll be rewarded by *his* grace for our charity."

But Marjory wasn't having it. "Rewarded with what?" she asked. "A bunch of criminals we can't feed. Hell. Estero ain't rich to begin with. Why not focus on our own issues?" To this, one of the ladies thanked Marjory for keeping an eye on fiduciary matters, and she recommended that the church engage in fundraising to sponsor the Cubans. But it was clear afterward that Marjory had crossed a line. The ladies didn't like her calling the Cubans criminals. When she was confronted one-on-one by Liz Anne, the group leader, she refused to apologize, and, in fact, she quit the group and the church altogether, which was really too bad.

Maybe if Marjory had stayed around longer, she would have had someone to talk to during those years when her husband's drinking turned full-blown trailer trash. Confined to their home and acreage, there was no neighbor in earshot who could hear the arguments they'd get into. Even on the sunniest days, Garth could get home from work and darken the whole sky. He was a force of nature—could bring the room down ten degrees. Sometimes, the man would sit out on the porch, firing his 12-gauge into the thunderstorms when she wouldn't put out. How she wished he'd just die. Once, he pinned her to the re-frigerator and, using a fillet knife, threatened to gut her like a fish if she didn't suck his dick. When she called the police, they came by— buddies of his—only to have drinks and a good laugh. If he hadn't disappeared in that hunting trip, God only knows what would have become of Marjory. This is why being site manager to the Immaculate Mulch Company was such an honor. It was an even greater honor to share in the company of men who respected her in her position. It hadn't come easy. She'd started as a temp driver when she was still in her early thirties, but she managed, as they say, to pull herself up, so that by the age of fifty-six, she was running the show.

Now, strolling onto her site, the sound of wood chippers buzzing in the distance filled her with joy. Maybe it was the pain meds, but all of the site looked absolutely luminous. The sun was reflecting off the machinery, and all around she could feel the deep warmth of the mulch radiating. Walking past the trailer, she could see the "We Appreciate You Very Mulch" banner, and she could smell the smoke and charcoal, which is why she was utterly surprised to see no one at the picnic tables.

That's not to say no one had attended the event; rather, it was as if the rapture had occurred.

The grill was wide open, burgers crisping. There were beer cans scattered about and already one vulture pecking at some uncooked hot dog meat—with the others looking on, standing in the shade, eyeing the roll-off containers further down the creek. *Devon! That boy can't do nothing right!* And just as she thought it, she saw him standing on one of the containers, keeping his balance, hands up, looking like one of those dumb inflatable things at the dealership, bending and dancing in the wind.

* * *

"Devon," she yelled, marching on over. "You get down from there right now!" He looked like a hoodlum, with his Immaculate Mulch polo a size too big and his baggy khakis all mud stained.

He grabbed the lip of the container and hopped down, and before she could reprimand him further, Tim Agee put his arm around her and said, "Marjory! Heard what happened. You okay?" The other men stepped away from the roll-off to check on her too. They looked giddy as schoolchildren come to see their mama. Seeing them all smiling and happy to be with her made her blush real hard. Maybe it was the pain meds, but for a moment, it all looked like it was happening in slow motion.

"Just a panther bite," she said, and she bit her tongue when she laughed.

"Oh," Tim said. "Just that, huh?"

"Food's getting burnt, boys," she said, sliding out from under Tim's arm and trying to redirect the crowd. "How's about we get that grill in order? Devon, what are you waiting on?"

Hank and Jeremy bowed their heads and started out back toward the picnic tables, but Charlie and Mike weren't budging. Neither was Tim. Marjory was getting ready to nudge them along again when something hissed and growled from inside the container. Sounded like a cross between a giant house cat and the demon Azazel himself. "What the fuck?" she said, and it was then, hearing the animal claw against the metal container, that she remembered she'd asked Rogelio to relocate the panther in there.

Mike, who was sporting a holster and handgun, said, "Quite a prize, Marjory."

"This prizeworthy to you?" she said, motioning to her bandages.

"I just never actually seen one before. It's big. It's a big motherfucker."

"I've seen 'em before," Tim said. "Seen them ravaging my chickens, those fuckers."

"I know. I know they're pests," she said.

"Well," Tim said, "how you plan on getting rid of it? It's not wise keeping it around like that."

"Go eat," she said and then, ignoring the men, proceeded to climb up on the rungs of the roll-off. She wanted to see the animal with her own eyes. And there it was, its face all bloody and dark in the Florida sun. It'd lost some of its goldish luster, that's for sure. Looked like a sticky booger with teeth. The creature was real sad looking, and gazing down upon it like the Lord herself, she almost felt bad for it. What she hadn't expected to find were empty beer cans scattered about the cat, a puddle of piss or beer or who knows gathering at the center of the rusty container. Of course, they'd had their fun with the cat. She was surprised that they hadn't killed it yet, all things considered.

One of those fuckers had eaten all of Hank's dogs, picked 'em off in a week alone: the shih tzu first, then the pug, and eventually the lab- radoodle. The way they hunted, the cats left no trace. If it wasn't for the security footage he kept on the property, he'd have never known. Mike had his beef too. He'd been driving down State Road 27 one evening when one of 'em ran out in front. Having seen all the Panther Crossing signs and all that, he knew better than to run it over, so he swerved and wrecked his car—drove it right into a concrete barricade; the airbags bruised his ribs bad.

Around these parts, folks didn't see eye to eye with the panther preservationist. What did it matter that some folks in Tallahassee or Miami or Washington felt compelled to save an animal already on the fast track to extinction? If it weren't for the steep penalties associated with harming the animal, surely their heads would already be hanging in people's living rooms. Though he didn't say it, Marjory could sense that's what Mike was after, eyeing the cat, gun in his holster.

In This World of Ultraviolet Light

Maybe Marjory should have trusted her gut, but she got distracted with that business of hosting these men. Before joining them at the cookout, she went to freshen up in the trailer; she even sprayed a bit of perfume. Who cared if it attracted a few bugs? By the time she made it back to the cookout, the grill was on fire and everyone was gone all over again. A beer-induced agreement had been struck in her absence. Her clients had decided that the panther needed to be fed into a wood chipper. They'd enlisted Devon, and thank God she hadn't been there to see that poor little black boy climb in the roll-off to shoo the panther out. What she did see was Charlie securing a chain around the creature's neck, then connecting that chain to one of the wheel loaders. She heard the screaming; it sounded like a woman. And she saw Tim drive the loader up to the mouth of her biggest wood chipper. What a fucking show. None of the Mexicans were working. All of 'em were standing around; they'd be holding their phones out, Instagramming, if the fuckers could afford it.

And the panther was really wailing. Mike kicked the shit out of its skull, and that shut it up for good. Marjory ran over to them, really feeling the pain now of where the creature had bitten her. Out of breath, she shoved Charlie and said, "You put it back! I didn't ask you all to do this shit."

"C'mon, Marjory. It's not like we was going to do it without you."

"Put it back," she said. "You got no right."

But nobody listened to her. Some Mexican fired up the wood chipper—the bright-red Rotochopper, the kind of machine that could eat up a whole forest without so much as a hiccup. Once it got mulching and those teeth started whirling and compacting, it felt like the whole site was just humming under Marjory's feet. Mike tossed an empty beer can into the wood chipper, and it screeched into a million pieces. Those tiny bits of aluminum got carried up the conveyer belt and shot out from the top of that long neck like confetti, straight to outer space. "Turn it off," she yelled. "Right now!" But nobody—not her clients, not her workers—could hear her shouting. And when the men each slouched to lift the dead animal and ease it into the wood chipper, something terrible overcame her. It had to be the medication. Because what she saw was not the panther at all. What she saw made her start pounding on Tim's arm, yelling, "Don't you see her? She's just a girl."

Marjory's yelling alarmed Tim so much that he stopped, and he said, "Girl? Marjory. Look for yourself. It's just a panther, a mangy swamp cat. The meds have you seeing things." This made sense. Of course it wasn't a human girl. Why would five grown men throw a girl in a wood chipper? But when she looked again, she cried because she couldn't unsee the girl: the white dress with the embroidered sunflowers; the wheat-colored sandals. It was *her,* wearing the same dress she'd worn when she had to accompany her husband on that hunting trip against her will. So when they tossed that vision of herself into the wood chipper, all the flesh and bone burst over the site into a fine mist, and Marjory gasped and grabbed her own skin as if the machine were, in fact, pulverizing her.

Some Mexican shut off the machine, and beyond the ringing in her ears, she could hear her clients laughing. And further away, near the site's office trailer, she could see something else: a white SUV with the green Florida Fish and Wildlife emblem emblazoned on the passenger door. Charlie wasn't laughing anymore. It rained a little blood, and he said, "Yup. I think we best be going now."

* * *

Devon ran on over and put out the grease fire, and the clients— the whole lot of them—slunk away, leaving Marjory to deal with the park ranger herself. Sure, Tim lingered about for a hot minute, scouring the earth for tiny bits of panther or any evidence that might somehow implicate him. Sure, there was some blood here and there and a bit of fur all caught in the wood chips, but it all blended in. Tim Agee must have felt good about himself because after he'd looked over the area, even wiped off a bit of blood from the Rotochopper with his finger, he grabbed onto his belt, looked up at the sky like some cowboy getting ready to pass through town, and walked off, didn't even say bye.

The site roared back to life, with workers taking to their shovels and movers. They were speaking in their language, probably gossiping; they were a bunch of mosquitoes buzzing about to the sound of grinders eating up trees and spitting out little colored pieces of wood. And

In This World of Ultraviolet Light

Marjory, seeing the inspector saunter over and nod hello to Tim, felt she needed a cry. What a day! It was as if she were *that* woman again, barefoot and watching a police car roll onto her property from a chink in the window blinds, her white dress covered in mud. So when the inspector greeted her, she flinched.

He was a Hispanic man, probably a Cuban 'cause his skin was lighter, and he seemed a tad more Americanized than the trash she dealt with day in and day out. In fact, he kind of looked like Ricky Martin, even had the same big pearly-white smile, except instead of living la vida loca, he was in tight green shorts and a white short-sleeve button-up, a radio in his over-the-shoulder holster. Seeing her flinch, he responded warmly, "Hi there, Marjory. I'm here to check in with you, okay?"

"And you think I'm Marjory?" she asked. "What? 'Cause I'm an old white woman?"

"No, ma'am. It's the bite. Doctors called it in. Figured it had to be you." And with that, the ranger introduced himself. "My name's Reinaldo, by the way. How's the bite feeling now?"

As he said this, he handed over his business card, and Marjory, stubborn as usual, said, "Bad. It's a bite."

"Can I see the panther?" he asked, looking over the property.

"You want to see it?"

"Yes, ma'am. It's why I'm here."

"Look," she said, "the fucker pounced on me. Had to shoot it."

Reinaldo smiled. "Ma'am, I'm not here to punish you."

"If saving my own life is a crime, then, fuck, I'm Charles Manson."

Reinaldo laughed. "I understand, and I want you to know that you got nothing to worry about. I would have shot the panther, too, if it'd attacked me. I don't think you're guilty."

"Thank you for saying that. It does give me some comfort," she said. "But I'm sorry to disappoint you. The panther was gone by the time I returned, and I'm glad it's gone. Workers said it ran off into the preserve, must have been two hours ago. You should go looking for it in there."

"You must be tired," Reinaldo said. "Please allow me to see the container you stored it in."

"Container?" Marjory rubbed her head. "You wouldn't believe how tired I am. I don't know. It was such a traumatic morning. Now you ask me where we kept the panther? Did we keep it?"

"Says so in the doctor's report," he said. He pulled out his phone, presumably searching for the document. "I'm looking for it now, but, in short, you told the doctors you were holding it."

"Like I said. Panther's gone. And those containers. They ain't just sitting around idle all day. We fill 'em up, transport 'em across the country. I wouldn't even know which one to direct you to."

"Well, if it did run off into the preserve, I'd still like to look around. Maybe track it."

"I guess that wouldn't hurt now. Least I could do," she said. "If you don't mind . . ."

"Ma'am," he said, "thank you for speaking with me. I hope you do get some rest."

Marjory nodded, and she went over to the picnic tables to have a seat. The whole area smelled of smoke and burnt food. How she wanted to get in her car and drive off for the day, but she wasn't about to leave until that man was off her property. So she watched him, feigning overseeing her multitude of workers, and when he knelt down in the mulch, only yards from the Rotochopper that had eaten the panther, he looked over at her, and she thought, *Oh, fuck,* and in that instant, lightning spread across the sky, followed, immediately, by the crack of thunder. It was enough to open up the heavens. Because right then and there, a downpour befell the whole of the facility, and Marjory, sitting under the trees, rejoiced in the rain and everything it would wash away.

* * *

It rained for three days and four nights. And because there was nothing worse than being on-site during rainstorms, Marjory did take sick time to tend her wounds. In the mornings, she'd unwrap the bandages and wipe the stink away. She'd marvel at the way the body knew to take care of itself, at the way her skin could regrow and encase her. The pain was becoming less. Sometimes she'd feel the memory of the bite, the weight and smell of the panther, so she'd take her meds and lie in bed.

When the panther tried to end her life, it maintained eye contact. It had such beautiful green eyes, just like his. Sometimes she missed him. Rarely. She tried not to think about the man she'd once loved, but it was hard not to. In the Fakahatchee Strand that day, he confronted her; he said, "What'd you think would happen, baby face, calling the cops?" He pulled out that fillet knife and cut her cheek, just so she'd know he could. "You know I love you," he whispered. And she embraced him because she thought he'd kill her right then and there. There was no question about it, in fact, and the more she remembered the events of that day, the less she wanted to linger at her house.

So, on the fourth day, Marjory returned to work because she was tired of being on meds. She was tired of having to live with the ghost of her husband. He was gone, but, fuck, his shit was everywhere. At night, she could still remember the sound of his breathing in the bedroom, deep. Even if she wasn't fully recovered, she was glad to be back on the site on a sunny day, the sky a brilliant azure. Already the migrant workers had gathered at the picnic tables like the hogs they are; there was garbage all over the place—a whole bin overflowing. But she didn't say nothing about it.

Because there was something else that had caught her attention. It was Reinaldo from the Department of Fish and Wildlife, still loitering on the site. She hadn't remembered seeing his truck on the way in. And now, watching him partake in coffee with all her Mexican laborers, a thought ripped through her mind: *Had her workers betrayed her? Had they snitched on Tim and Charlie and the whole lot of 'em?* In an instant, she could see it: her best clients implicated in a federal crime; reporters swarming the facility, asking for each gory detail. She could picture how all the notice would inevitably draw the attention of ICE. What would happen to her migrant workforce? Would they all be deported? Maybe it was paranoia, but seeing Reinaldo in his green ranger gear and his big-ass stupid smile, like a green viper embedded among his prey, made Marjory certain she was doomed.

The men, who typically were quite solemn so early in the morning, were engaged in a deep conversation with Reinaldo. The chatter was unbearable. It made her feel like an outsider on her own site. She felt that beautiful morning like she might have been in some Spanish-speaking country. The words, once uttered, emerged from deep within the men like locusts; they swarmed the trees and the mounds of mulch; they were the kinds of words that could tear through the civilized world, right down to the bone. Fucking Reinaldo; he'd pandered to them. He'd pretended: *I'm Latino just like you.* But Marjory knew better. Those government folks loved no one, so she confronted the man.

She marched right up to her workers and shouted, "This ain't no social hour. Get to work," and so the men did, packing up their things and rushing off. In the midst of all that movement, Reinaldo didn't budge. "And you?" Marjory said. "Why are you harassing my workers?"

"Harassing?" he said. "I assure you, ma'am, that is not the case at all."

"They won't speak to you," she said.

"I know. It's a common problem. They think I'm here to deport them. Look, I'm Latino too. I wouldn't dream of reporting these folks to ICE. Maybe you could communicate that for me."

To this, Marjory sat across from him. She had to sit because she could feel her body betraying her: the increased heartbeat. She was breathing heavy, even, and trying to hide it.

"Why bother?"

"One of them did say that it wasn't you that shot the panther." Reinaldo looked over his notes as he spoke. "Come to think of it, if you were the one attacked, how would you have time to turn a shotgun on the panther?" He motioned with his hands, as if he were holding a weapon. He seemed, to Marjory, to be reenacting the ordeal in his mind. "It happened right here, right?"

"It did," she said. "Right by the creek. Fucker jumped out of a tree."

"And then one of your workers took the gun and shot the panther."

"No," she said, "I did it."

"Ma'am. You don't have to protect no one. I just need to understand what happened. Every time one of these panthers winds up dead, there's plenty of paperwork I got to fill out. Help me out."

Marjory didn't trust this ranger for a second. He was a sly motherfucker. She could feel his questions closing in on her. Every time he asked a question or for help, she sensed he already knew the answer. Sitting across from him, watching the man take notes, she was certain that in the days she'd been away, he'd spoken to every single one of her workers. And, of course, her men would have implicated her by now. They'd seen what happened; they'd seen the panther get turned to mulch, and they'd seen who'd done it. And hadn't the ranger, that day after the incident, kneeled down to pick up a bit of the panther from the ground? What had he found? A bit of hair? A tooth? So, rather than playing this game and feigning ignorance, Marjory just came out with it. "And did my workers," she asked, "tell you where the body is? Tell me, has anyone taken the time to show you?"

"The body? Is it dead?"

"Kid, don't insult my intelligence."

"You said it ran off into the preserve. So you were lying?"

"I can take you to it if you like."

"Sure," he said. "I'd love to see it."

* * *

Marjory slung the shotgun over her shoulder. She enlisted the help of her intern and handed him a shovel, and together with the ranger, they crossed the creek into the preserve. They walked until they could no longer hear the sounds of the mulch machines. Devon complained the whole way, and he was suspicious as hell, but Marjory reminded him that if he wanted his A, he'd best comply.

This far from the site, there was only the faint trickle of water, the wind in the leaves, and the buzzing of insects. As such, nobody spoke; they only moved through the rock and mud, blazing through grass, heading to what Marjory would consider far enough. "Far enough yet?" she'd asked her husband when he'd taken her out on that hunting trip. She was certain he was going to kill her, and maybe he would have, except he stopped to pee this one time—big, strong, pungent stream— and she'd taken the 12-gauge, which he'd left leaning against a tree. He laughed real good, and she put it to the back of his head. It blasted a hole in his skull. Scared all the birds away. It was as if she'd taken all his bullshit—the smashing of plates, the hitting and shouting and name-calling, the constant need to get off on her, even when she didn't want to—and she tucked it in that sorry-looking body of his so that every critter in the world could have a go at it. How good it felt to drag his body into the waterway, to be done with him, to donate him and his flesh to the gators.

Now, she could remember that the gators didn't lunge at his body right away. They were skeptical lizards, swimming about, nudging it. It was the vultures that started on him first. With every bit of him that they ate, she felt the tension leaving her. By the time the gators dragged him under and ripped him apart, she was a new woman; she felt good about herself, killing that fucker. Maybe she'd been reborn on that day, transformed from a domestic violence victim to someone who could manage the whole of Immaculate Mulch without batting an eyelash, to someone with power.

It's what she planned on doing now to the ranger. They walked until they found a clearing of saw grass and stone. And would you believe it? In that clearing, there were two panther cubs; they looked like overgrown kittens, sand colored with black spots. Devon saw them first. "Look, Marjory. Look how cute."

And then Reinaldo smiled, and he knelt by the cubs, who were shy. "I don't believe it. Cubs in the wild," he said. "They must be separated. They must be hungry." And so Reinaldo used his water bottle to offer them drinking water; the cubs came out, lapped it up, and that's when Marjory put the gun against his head, just as she had done before. She put the gun there because she needed to end this business with the panther once and for all, and she knew, even when the ranger had assured her he'd dropped the investigation, that he'd lied; he was onto her.

The cubs didn't run when he collapsed on the mud. Sure, they flinched, but it only took a minute or so before one of them ambled over and licked some of Reinaldo's flesh. Devon, watching the little cubs chew on that man's brain, said, "Shit! What the fuck?"

And Marjory, looking at those little cubs, wasn't sure what to do: *Should she exterminate them too, or should she let them live?* And feeling a maternal instinct, she put her hand on Devon's shoulder and said, "Let 'em eat. Then we'll bury it."

"I'm not gonna . . ."

"Yes, you are," she said, "or I'll call the cops myself, and, well, you understand."

Devon nodded.

In This World of Ultraviolet Light

So, that's what they did. They watched the little cubs clean the flesh off the bone, and when the cubs were satisfied, when their little mouths were stained, they cleaned themselves with their tongues while Devon dug a hole. It was hard work, digging in the marsh. Not much soil. The whole landscape was just a bit of filth atop ancient coral. By the time the ranger had been buried, the cubs were asleep, and Marjory, feeling the sun on her skin and smelling the mud and algae, said, "I can see now why we protect it." A mosquito landed on her arm, bit her, and she let it. She watched its belly fill with her blood, and she was grateful for it—for what her blood would do to its little eggs.

8

Obsolescence

My grandmother says she was born in the clouds, a thousand feet above Hiroshima. She remembers the womb, her ear against the cold carbide case, listening to the whip of *Enola Gay*'s propellers. She remembers falling. Even now she parts her hair to show me the keloid scars on her head and explains that she was merely crowning when the mandorla burned up. "It was a cruel way to enter this world," she says. "But when I opened my eyes, I knew everything that had ever been and everything that would ever be."

* * *

We lived west of Miami. For a long time, our home was on a prairie at the far edge of Miami. I didn't really know the city, but I knew that its lights made the sky look like rust. Our front yard faced a field of slash. The backyard was an oasis—a two-acre mango grove cultivated by my grandfather. The grove was fenced in by hedges that protected the delicate mango flowers from the gusts. There was a shed at the heart of the grove where my grandfather raised lories. Sometimes other birds visited the lories—herons, anhingas, ibises. A statue of Michael slaying Lucifer protected the shed, its base sealed with candle wax and rose petals. During the Christmas season, my grandmother wrapped the statue in multicolored lights, and we'd sit outside, wishing for snow and talking about the past.

* * *

Men used to ride through these prairies at night. On hot summer nights when the air conditioner would freeze over, we sat on the porch, watching their outlines cross us at dusk; the embers of their cigars were like the beacons of airplanes flying overhead.

My grandfather sat beside a carton of mangos, his dentures on his lap, hoping an opportunity to trade would arise. What he wanted was turtle meat. He believed the Miccosukee could get him the meat. Though he'd never chewed turtle meat before, he knew it to be aphrodisiacal. He'd caught many turtles before, but something about ripping the turtle from its shell didn't agree with him. My grandmother said it was because he was a pendejo. "Just enough mangos to save your own life. You selfish old man. What if the Miccosoukees come and want to take away your grandson? What would you do then?"

"Don't be crazy. It's for the turtle meat. Indians aren't like that."

"Turtle meat. Turtle meat. Turtle meat."

"Stop that, Helga. Do we have to pick at each other all the time?"

And she'd form her hand into the shape of a bird's beak and pick at his side. Then she'd laugh and tell me stories, her adventures fighting Indians in Cuba.

"That's what you don't know. Those Cuban Injuns are good-for-nothing—the worst kinds of pigs: pigs that steal pigs. They'll steal your pigs before you even know it. Those pigs used to steal our pigs all the time. They'd come down from the mountains and take everything but the pig heads, so all we'd find were a bunch of pig heads in the morning.

So you know what I did? I killed them. I tied a red stocking around my head, like Mr. Rambo. When they climbed into that pen, I launched up out of the mud and scared the pigs out of them. I shot them. Then I snapped their necks, chopped them up with a machete, and fed them to the pigs. All I left were those pigs' heads, and I left their heads along the pigpen enclosure as a warning to the rest of those pigs. That year, the pigs were nice and fat, and we ate well. Pigs will eat anything if you let them, you know? They'd even eat you, mi amor."

"You're scaring the poor child," my grandfather would say, slicing and peeling open a mango. He'd caress my crown and offer a golden cube, but I didn't eat mango then; I was more interested in his dentures. For a long time, I was convinced there was some sort of release latch in my mouth that would allow me to remove my teeth also.

* * *

When I was a child, I didn't have an appetite. My grandmother had to be clever in order to feed me. She'd take me on lizard-hunting expeditions in the grove to distract me. Every time I'd catch a lizard, she'd sneak a spoonful of rice into my mouth. Then she'd take the lizard from my hands, snap its neck, and toss it over the hedges.

"Do we have to kill them?" I'd say, my mouth full of rice.

"What? You feel bad for a lizard?"

"Well, yeah."

"Well, don't be like your grandfather, mi amor. Let's find another one."

Eventually, we weren't so much concerned with brown and green anoles. Those were clumsy lizards, quick to defecate. Plus, they'd lose their tails when we'd catch them. It was the Cuban knights we searched for—the noble, vicious, and venomous lizards. We'd shake them off the trees. Then my grandmother would let me beat them with a broom until I'd broken their legs or paralyzed them. When they could hardly move, she'd snap their necks and toss them over the hedges also. Then she'd force a spoonful of rice into my mouth and say, "You'll need your strength for the next battle, mi amor."

After I'd grown accustomed to eating rice, she tried to get me hooked on meat, so she'd mince flank steak and hide the bits under a plate of rice and diced mango. She'd feed me as we hunted for knights,

In This World of Ultraviolet Light

but I'd sift the meat and the mango out with my tongue, and I'd form these giant flavorless balls of meat and hide them between my teeth and cheeks. She'd reach into my mouth and fling them over the hedges. "Here you are throwing away perfectly good food," she'd say. "Meanwhile, Fidel Castro is drinking horse milk. He's getting closer to the secret of my powers, you know?"

"What powers?"

And she'd interrupt me by shoving another spoonful into my mouth.

* * *

That one month in the summer when the storms knock all the mangos to the ground and the sun turns the pulp to yellow jelly so that the yard is buzzing with horseflies, my grandmother and I would clean the yard, shoveling mangos into a wheelbarrow. We'd push the wheelbarrow over to the hedges and spend the afternoon flinging them over. Occasionally, she'd cup a handful of jelly and try to shove it in my mouth. I'd have to bite her fingers to make her stop. Concerned I might spill over under heatstroke, she'd pour cups of ice water over my head. In retaliation, I'd hose her down. By the end of the day, we'd be soaked and covered in mango pulp, and she'd curse at my grandfather for all his planting: "Your trees are going to be the death of me."

* * *

When I was eleven, my grandfather began raising birds for a living. He spoke bird. All it took was a few whistles and caws, and he'd have any bird eating mango out of his hand. He started out with lovebirds but upgraded to lories. One Easter, he seduced a peacock into the yard and trapped it in his toolshed. Convinced trapping a peacock was bad luck, my grandmother snuck into the toolshed with me. She handed me a broom, shoved me.

"Why don't we let it go?" I said.

"Because if we let it go, he will whistle and hold out some mango and catch it again. He always catches them again."

"We can blindfold it and take it far away and release it in a nice place it will never want to leave."

"It will return," she said. "All birds end up here."

She poked at the broom and asked, "Are you going to do it?"

Before I could answer, she grabbed the peacock by its neck. The lories went nuts—cawing and beating their wings against the cages. I had to cover my ears to bear their high-pitched shrieks. They sounded like sirens. Their shrieks were ringing and digging into my skull, so I thought I might cry their cries. I was going to step out of the shed, but she slammed the door shut, looked at me. The curls of her hair were plastered against her face with sweat. She lifted that peacock over her head. Then she twisted its neck as if it were dough. She was spinning the bird over her head, slamming it into the spades and shovels and pickaxes affixed to the ceiling. It rained red and green feathers. When she dropped the bird on the ground, it lay gray and limp, and she laughed. It was an embarrassed laugh. She'd gotten carried away and made a mess, and she knew it. Stuck to the blood-splotched shed walls were the peacock's feathers, which made it seem like we were being watched by a thousand blue eyes.

We spent the afternoon cleaning the shed, careful to remove all the feathers. She threw the peacock over the hedges. The following day, when my grandfather asked what had happened to the peacock, my grandmother shrugged and said, "It must have escaped."

"Helga," he said, "leave my birds alone."

"Be quiet, old man."

* * *

The red lories were known to attract pests, so my grandfather purchased a cat named Kitty. There was an open lanai, and sometimes Kitty would leave snakes or birds as offerings on the welcome mat by the screen door in exchange for a can of tuna. Occasionally, I'd poke Kitty's offerings with a stick, which my grandmother could not tolerate. She'd curse, "Coño. Carajo," and fling the dead animals over the hedges. Then she'd beat Kitty with a broom, and my grandparents would argue about the proper ways to treat animals.

When Kitty vanished, it seemed natural then that everything should end up flung over the hedges at one point or another. Sometimes at dusk I'd climb over the hedges, careful not to prick myself, and I'd play in the prairie. I'd pretend I was an archeologist looking for dinosaurs, and I'd dig up the bones of all the lizards and snakes we'd thrown over the hedges for all those years. There were many. Kitty was there, and so was the peacock. Sometimes I'd poke at Kitty's bones. But I'd leave the bird bones alone. Something about the way birds decompose, whirled about their feathers, reminded me of angels.

It was lonely on the other side of the hedges. How I wished there was someone to help me unearth all these bones.

* * *

The excavators arrived the summer I finished middle school. The sparse trees were removed. Pits were dug all over the prairie and filled with water. Roads that led to nowhere were laid. At night, we'd sleep to the rumbling of distant dynamite, and I'd imagine Florida's limestone crust ripping open, revealing its primordial pulp.

I remember when the famous community developer, Escalado, knocked on our door. My grandfather generously offered him a bucket of complimentary mangos. Escalado had come to place an offer on our home—half a million dollars. My grandparents declined. Perhaps if he'd included turtle meat in his offer, he'd have received a warmer reception.

Escalado named the prairie Mango Lakes. Even though he was known to be wealthy, for a long time he lived in a trailer surrounded by excavators and limestone rubble. In the trailer there were three miniature model homes and watercolored sketches of what he imagined Mango Lakes would look like—there would always be a sunset. But our home was not in Escalado's vision. "He'd have to choke on it," my grandmother said.

* * *

I started choking the chicken, or pulling the weasel, tugging the turtle, snapping the lizard's neck, doing the five-knuckle shuffle— whatever it is people call it these days—at around the time my grandparent's unofficial dumpsite was purchased. The new owners, a family of Indians, converted that section of their land into a private pool, the kind that has those petrified cherubs pissing into it. Townhomes were erected around the yard, and before long, the rats and the snakes were gone. But my grandmother continued flinging things over the hedges as if nothing had changed at all.

Neighbors sitting on their second-story balconies watched her litter their yards with rotten fruit or the severed heads of holiday pigs. Seldom was there a knock at the door or a complaint. Sometimes neighbors simply threw the heads back, but mostly the neighbors quietly dealt with the inconvenience.

On those long afternoons, which should have been dedicated to catching up on high school summer reading lists, I'd sit by my bedroom window and watch Jen Osceola swim. She was the daughter of the Indians who'd moved in next door, and watching her swim would make me stiff as a diving board. She had this long, dark hair that would trail behind her breaststrokes like the train of a wedding dress.

Her parents would call out to her: "Jennifer. Come inside. Dinner's almost ready." While my grandmother watered the trees below, I'd watch Jen climb out of the pool, dripping wet. But my grandmother would catch me peeking through the curtains, so she'd hose down my window; all I'd see were the refractions of light in her blasts of water.

* * *

That one month before school goes back into session, when it rains every afternoon and the hurricanes dance off Florida's coast, I'd help my grandmother tape giant Xs onto the major windows—even if there wasn't a storm coming. "Better to be prepared," she'd say, although I wasn't sure how tape would protect glass from a hurricane.

"How about hurricane shutters?" I asked.

"Tape is fine."

"Shutters can block debris," I said. "They can protect us better."

"Mi amor. Don't be like your grandfather."

So I'd help her carry the statue of Michael slaying Lucifer into the shed. Then we'd carry in all the aluminum yard furniture and all the crap my grandfather had accumulated over the years. The lories would shriek when we'd enter the shed, and she'd slam her palm against their cages and verbally remind them about the peacock.

* * *

In This World of Ultraviolet Light

In 1992, the summer before my senior year, it rained terribly, and we had one hurricane, Andrew, which might have killed us all had it not veered south toward Homestead. Winds blew against our home at over two hundred miles per hour for nearly a day. It sounded like a train was ratcheting by the house, scraping against the walls.

When the hurricane passed, we learned Andrew had taken the birds' shed. It was raining red feathers. We also learned he'd smashed one of our Xs in the guest bedroom. Part of the roof had lifted off, and it seemed the ceiling had oozed its guts like a rotten mango—orange foam, soaked and dripping onto the carpet. The carpet was infested with flies, so the door to this room was shut and sealed off for weeks.

The entire neighborhood lost electricity, which made nights difficult. With no AC, we slept in our underwear on the hall tiles with all the windows open. My grandmother would leave one candle lit, and if I needed to use the bathroom, I'd have to take the candle with me. I'd never examined our home under candlelight. The simplest objects—a hand-carved turtle my grandfather bought in the Dominican Republic, a photo of him playing guitar for my young grandmother—vibrated under its light. Shadows ran from my field of vision, so wherever I placed the candle changed my perception of things.

During the days, my grandfather walked to the general stores on Tamiami Trail and waited for shipments of ice, which wouldn't come for a long time. My grandmother and I cleared debris from the yards: part of a satellite dish, shingles from the neighbor's roof, panels of plywood and branches. We'd pile this all up by the side of the road. Then we'd sit at the kitchen counter, and I'd watch her eat the only thing available, mangos.

* * *

Helping her fling bunches of mango skin over the hedges, I wondered how the Osceolas were faring. From my window, I could see their pool had been drained. The cherubs were gone. There was a silver box powered up on the side of their house, and I realized, under careful observation, their windows were closed. Their air conditioner was working.

That evening I told my grandparents about the Osceola family's AC. My grandfather brought out his mango buckets. My grandmother helped him fill them. We walked around the block and to their house. It was the only house that had its lights on. Something about having the porch light on seemed gluttonous in our hurricane aftermath.

My grandparents were afraid to ring the doorbell, so I did. Jen answered. She was dressed in a Dolphins football jersey and matching sweatpants. She had a blue beeper clipped on her waistband. Her hair was wet and braided, and she was holding a Nintendo controller in her hand.

"Hi," I said.

She smiled.

"Get your father. We would like to trade," my grandmother said. She plopped down the bucket of mangos. "The best," she said with a sweep of her hand.

"There's nothing to trade except electricity," Jen said. She reached into the bucket and took a mango. Her father came to the door and invited us in. My grandparents followed him into the living room with their buckets, to count mangos, I suppose. I sat on the floor next to Jen, facing the television and feeling the cool AC blowing over me.

"Do you play a lot of Nintendo?" I asked.

"Not really. Now it's the only thing to do."

"What do you do then?"

"When the pool isn't drained, I swim," she said, though she was more inclined to play Mario Bros. than talk.

After a moment of awkward silence, I asked, "You swim professionally?"

She didn't answer. She'd just gotten a star. She was glowing and radiating and running through the desert, killing every turtle in sight. When she reached the end of the level, she jumped up on the flagpole, and as she slid to its base, the points were counted off. "One up," she said, and she laughed. "What do you think of that? Bet you can't do better." So she handed me the control, and we played through the night, dying a lot.

Around midnight, Jen took another mango, sliced a piece of it for her and another for me. I shook my head and said, "I really don't eat mango."

"Who doesn't eat mango? Try it."

In This World of Ultraviolet Light

"Maybe another time."

"But this one is really good," she said. "You have to try this one." She held the mango in front of my face. I could smell it. Iron, I thought. My grandmother walked into the room, saving me. So Jen ate the slice.

Then my grandmother sat next to us because it was time to go. She said, "You two would make wonderful babies."

"Helga," I said.

Jen laughed and scooted away from me. "Your grandmother is crazy."

That night as I lay on the hall tile under the glow of the Osceola home listening to the breeze in the mango trees, I wished the electricity would never come back. Feeling the breeze blow on me, I wanted to pleasure myself while thinking of her. I went to the kitchen and sliced a piece of mango into the shape of her lips. I returned to the tile floor and set those cold lips on my own. Juice dripped down my face, some into my mouth.

I thought of Jen's wet hair braided, its knobs dragging along my skin. I bit into the mango, sucked on its pulp. I thought of her laughter every time she'd run into a Koopa Troopa or fall in a hole. It was radiant. I imagined going for a swim with her sometime and being so stiff it would hurt, and I swallowed the fruit and reached for her, but something kept pulling me away because then I'd think of the peacock choking and its bones poking us in the pool. I'd hear the red lories shriek, and peacock feathers would bubble to the surface. Dynamite would rumble in the distance. Jen would be swimming away, trying to get away from the excavators, her dark hair following her like the train of a wedding dress, and I'd see my grandmother standing over us holding a bowl of shredded meat and rice and conjuring up what only she and her powers could foresee.

ACKNOWLEDGMENTS

I am grateful for the support that I received from the Cuba One Foundation, the Kimmel Harding Nelson Center, the Santa Fe Writer's Conference, the Sewanee Writer's Conference, the Sundress Academy for the Arts, and the Ithaca College Pre-Doctoral Diversity Fellowship. Much gratitude to the editors at *Indiana Review*, Indiana University Press, and Anjali Sachdeva, as well as the following publications, in which these stories appeared, in slightly different form:

"All along the Hills," *Sonora Review* 69 (2016): 36–37.
"Ropa Vieja," *Alimentum: The Literature of Food* (May 2014).

"Never through Miami," *Greensboro Review* 106 (2019): 28–46.

"The Roasting Box," *Cossack Review* 2.1 (2014): 39–41.

"Stand Your Ground," *Hayden's Ferry Review* 69 (2022): 150–159.

"The Phone Thieves," *Tenemos* (Spring 2015): 47–55.

"Obsolescence," *Saw Palm: Florida Literature & Art* 7 (2013): 22–39.

To Eleanor Henderson, Jack Wang, and Jacob White, my friends and colleagues at Ithaca College. To Nick White and to Xavier Navarro, for their friendship and generosity. And to my agent and first editor, Jane von Mehren, whose feedback and care has made me a better writer.

To my wife, Mixalicha Moriaux. This collection exists because during the subprime mortgage crises, she encouraged me to return to school and pursue a career in writing, and later when I was pursuing a graduate education in writing and publishing while still working for a vacuum cleaner company, she insisted that I quit and focus all my attention on my studies. She was able to imagine a path forward when I could not. She is my first reader. And to my daughter, Olivia Palma, who at eight years old helped me realize the ending of "Immaculate Mulch."

RAUL PALMA is the author of *A Haunting in Hialeah Gardens*. He is a member of the fiction faculty in Ithaca College's Department of Writing. He earned his PhD in English at the University of Nebraska, with a specialization in ethnic studies. He lives in Ithaca, New York.